The

on the

Brighton

Train

by Kim Mede

To my English teacher and to my favourite
authors - thank you.

❖

CHAPTER ONE

The first news bulletin came courtesy of the precise, clipped tones of the BBC's male radio announcer:

"Dora Jenkins, former ballerina with the Royal Ballet, has died at the age of 82. Miss Jenkins was discovered yesterday in her home in Lower Broadwood, Midfordshire. She apparently succumbed to heart failure during the night.

Dora Jenkins was born in Suffolk in 1871. At the age of three, she told her mother that she wanted to be a ballerina. She studied with several ballet companies in her teens and early twenties and made her debut in the chorus of Swan Lake in 1891. The impresario Ivan Petrovski described her as..."

❖

Detective Chief Inspector Joseph Brookland listened attentively to his Sergeant's report. From where he stood in the hallway, he could see into the tidy sitting room and watch his gloved officers carefully searching through the bureau drawers, and in and around the room's other furniture and furnishings. A tall man of forty-seven years, with thinning black hair and a small, neat moustache, Brookland gave his attention to his younger colleague: a slim, handsome, blond man of thirty-four. Both were attired in hats and raincoats; although it was early June, there had been thunderstorms until recently, and the weather was still unsettled.

'The old lady's body was in her chair and the wireless was on, as if she had died listening to the news,' Detective Sergeant Robert Collins said quietly, as if speaking too loudly would awaken the corpse. 'The pathologist anticipated heart failure until Mrs Jenkins' nurse pointed out that the old lady had apparently already been to bed, being in her nightgown and robe, and would never get up again to listen to the wireless. That's why she dialled '999', and not the local doctor's number. Smart girl,' the Sergeant said, obviously impressed.

'Indeed. Were there any signs of violence on the body?'

'Not at first sight. The coroner will have to determine actual cause of death, but as you can see, I have the men checking for anything that could help us discover what happened. I've had the photographer take pictures of this room and outside, and the kitchen.'

'What about suspects, motive?' enquired Brookland. 'Is there anything that someone might want to steal?' He glanced around the room but saw nothing to indicate Miss Jenkins was wealthy, but he knew from experience that lack of expensive possessions didn't preclude a large bank account.

'The nurse had plenty of opportunities,' said Collins, indicating the young woman in conversation with a WPC in the kitchen. 'But having pointed out to us that what might have been a natural death could be suspicious, it doesn't make much sense she'd kill her employer and then alert us to the odd circumstance of her death, does it? Then there's a nephew; he hasn't been seen recently, either by the nurse or the neighbours. That's assuming there is anything valuable to steal,' he added as an afterthought, and then continued. 'There's also a local gardener who comes by twice a week to keep the garden tidy.'

'Let's see if the nurse can tell us about Miss Jenkins' finances. We can check her employer's finances later.' Brookland said, 'What is her name?'

'Eve Gillespie.'

Brookland walked into the kitchen and the two women seated at the table stopped their conversation to look at him.

'Nurse Gillespie? I'm Detective Chief Inspector Brookland. Do you feel capable of answering some questions about Miss Jenkins?'

'I think so, Chief Inspector.' Eve Gillespie looked to be around twenty-two years of age, with dark, wavy hair and of average height, with a generous figure. She looked composed, but the handkerchief in her hand told of her distress. Her companion, supportive and reassuring, was one WPC Louise Harris, twenty-eight, slim, with shoulder-length brown hair now pinned under her hat. Louise lightly touched her hand to Eve's arm. Eve looked first at her, then back to the Chief Inspector. He came around the table to sit in the chair across from her. DS Collins hung back at the kitchen door. Harris watched both men in turn, familiar with both their postures and their ways of working.

'What time did you find her? Brookland began.

'Around five past eight.'

'When did you last see Miss Jenkins alive?'

'At around nine-thirty Friday night. Miss Jenkins was ready for bed, so I turned down the covers and she got in. I said goodnight, turned off the upstairs lights and went back downstairs. I turned off the hall lights and let myself out of the front door. I tugged on it to check it was secure. It was.'

'Did you see anybody in the street?

'No, nobody.'

'You walked to the bus stop?'

'No, my young man drove me home. He waited by the gate and we left in his car.'

'And his name?'

'James Bracewell. He's a journalist with the

local paper.' She smiled slightly.

'Does he always drive you home?'

'No, he's often busy in the evenings, so I catch the bus home, but he usually picks me up on Fridays. We just have time for a drink in the pub.'

The Inspector looked up at Collins, who was busy making notes of the interview, and then back at Eve.

'You say Miss Jenkins never came back into the sitting room once she had gone to bed?'

'That's right, Inspector. The bathroom is upstairs if she needs to use it. She doesn't... didn't like to use the stairs at night, in case she fell. When I saw her in her chair, I was shocked! I knew something wasn't right, so I dialled '999' straight away...'

'Very glad you did, Miss.' Brookland stood up and walked to his Sergeant, gesturing him outside into the hallway.

'Have you checked for forced entry into the house?'

Collins nodded. 'There's no sign of a break-in around the doors or windows...'

'Sarge?' A man's voice interrupted. A young man in a grey suit and light raincoat beckoned to him from the kitchen and pointed into the now-open pantry. Collins and Brookland joined him.

'What is it, Dale?'

'The pantry window has been accessed from the

outside and re-closed. There are damp prints from a shoe on the lino.'

❖

The DCI looked into the pantry and took a pace inside, taking care not to disturb the area around the prints. Collins looked, but stayed at the entrance. The pantry was a small, deep cupboard perhaps four feet by five, shelved on three levels to a depth of around fifteen inches to allow room for a person to access each shelf. The shelves were stacked with packets and tins, some kitchen equipment and various knick-knacks for use by the household. A large sash window faced onto the garden, and a metal air vent kept the room cold.

The floor area was partly clear with a pair of square wooden stools and a few large crates containing fresh produce on one side. On the opposite side of the room were two pairs of outdoor boots of different sizes and styles, both feminine in style, presumably belonging to the victim. A storm lamp stood nearby. Also, on the floor of the pantry, in the centre in front of the window, was a clear toe-print and several smudged footprints as if someone had come in from the outside and left again by the same means. A fragment of leaf lay on the floor near one of the prints. The shelf below the window bore traces of shoe marks and the window fastener was not closed.

Collins tapped his commanding officer on the shoulder and pointed to one side of a lower shelf.

'Sir,' he spoke quietly, 'those biscuits look as if they have been disturbed.' He pointed to a plate of uneven and obviously homemade produce, slightly off centre as if some had been removed.

Brookland nodded. 'Ask Nurse Gillespie to step this way for a moment, Sergeant.' Collins disappeared, only to reappear a moment later with the nurse in tow.

'Nurse Gillespie,' Brookland addressed the young woman, 'these biscuits appear to have been disturbed. Were they like this the last time you entered? Please don't touch anything.' He partly blocked the doorway, forcing the nurse to peer around him to see where he was indicating.

'How odd. I'm sure they were arranged neatly when I left last night. I brought them from home, in a tin, but I needed the tin so I left them on the plate instead. Miss Jenkins had one with her tea, I had one too, so that should have left eight. There's only six now... perhaps one of your officers took them?'

Brookland stiffened. 'They know better than to touch anything.'

I hope, he thought to himself.

'Could you take a look around and see if anything else is missing? Did Miss Jenkins own anything valuable, something a thief might want to steal - jewellery, perhaps?'

He suspected the answer would be 'no', but the

nurse started at his words, and said, 'Her jewellery was nothing special, but she did have some interesting decorated plates and a few vases she inherited from her family. I believe some of them were quite unusual. They're in the sitting room.'

Brookland looked at Collins, who nodded. He had watched as the body had been removed from the sitting room by attendants.

'My men should be finished in there for the present if you feel able to go into that room?'

'I think so, Chief Inspector. I am used to people dying.' Eve countered, drawing herself up as straight as she could.

'I realise that, Nurse Gillespie, but not usually in that way, I'm sure.'

Eve nodded. 'You need my help, Chief Inspector. I'll be fine.' She turned and walked down the hallway into the sitting room. She paused at the door, but went in. Brookland and Collins followed behind her. Eve took one look around the room, then headed for the shelves against one wall. She frowned and turned back to the two police officers.

'There's one missing, I'm sure there is. A short blue vase.'

Collins approached the shelf to look for himself. 'Where did it sit?'

Eve pointed between two plates. 'It was right there yesterday.'

Collins stared at the shelf. Brookland came up beside him; Eve backed out of his way and stood to one side.

'What is it?'

'No dust.' Collins spun around and addressed Eve. 'Did you or Miss Jenkins dust this shelf recently?'

Eve frowned and shook her head. 'Miss Jenkins can't reach and I haven't touched the shelf for a week or so. It should be a little dusty...' She stepped forward and Collins ran a finger over the shelf, then showed it to her. There was no dust on his finger.

'Oh!' she said.

'Someone has removed the vase and dusted the shelf, then moved the remaining items to disguise the space,' Brookland said. 'Someone who came in through the pantry window, and probably left the same way, helping himself to biscuits.' He turned to Eve once more.

'Can you give me a description of the vase?' He looked at Collins, who turned over a new page in his notebook.'

'It was short, quite broad around, about this big.' The nurse indicated a size of around eight inches in circumference and around six inches high. 'It was a baby blue ceramic vase, quite attractive. I don't know what it was worth - perhaps her nephew could tell you?'

Eve looked at Collins, who consulted his notebook before looking at Brookland. 'Mr Edward Jenkins, solicitor with Davis and Prout in Wringford.'

'Partner.' Eve corrected him.

'We'll talk to him later today.' Brookland turned back to Eve. 'Who else has access to this house, Nurse Gillespie?'

'There's the gardener: his name is John Miller. He lives nearby. He doesn't have a telephone, so you'll have to send one of your men to fetch him.' Eve said brightly. 'But I doubt he killed Miss Jenkins,' she added.

'And why would you think that, Miss?' Brookland queried. 'Because he was fond of the old lady?'

'Because he couldn't fit through the window. And he doesn't eat biscuits.'

Brookland despatched a constable to the address given by Nurse Gillespie. Around fifteen minutes later, a tall thickset man in his mid-fifties, dressed in a tweed jacket, black trousers and flat cap walked up to the front door, followed by the constable sent to find him. Brookland nodded to his man who resumed his post outside the house. He moved towards Miller and extended his hand, which the newcomer cautiously shook.

'Mr Miller, I apologise for disturbing your Saturday, but I need to ask you questions about your movements since yesterday.'

Miller frowned. 'What for? Your constable said there'd been a burglary here last night. If Miss Jenkins thinks I stole something, she's mistaken. Where is she? Let me talk to her.'

'She's dead, Mr Miller. She had a heart attack last night.'

Miller's jaw dropped. He swallowed hard. 'Oh, God. Oh, the poor lady. I didn't realise— I apologise for my words just now. I thought... I don't understand. Your constable told me she'd been burgled. Was that true?'

'It was. We believe she disturbed the thief trying to steal something from this room. The resulting strain caused her heart to give out.'

'Oh, poor Miss Jenkins. What would anyone want to steal here? Did she have money or valuable rings or suchlike? I've seen her wearing some pretty trinkets that might appeal to some. And there's a dinner service that's very fancy, all gold edging. And a set of gold-plated teaspoons, a presentation from the Ballet Company, she said. Or maybe...'

'We're looking into that now,' said Brookland, eager to stem Miller's imagination before he inventoried the entire house. 'Where were you last evening, Mr Miller?'

'In the 'Three Ferrets' until closing time, then home. The wife can say the same. She fetched me home. She'll tell you I slept all night, woke me up for breakfast at half-past eight.'

'And when did you last see Miss Jenkins?'

Miller thought for a moment, staring past Brookland, then looking at him once more. 'Yesterday afternoon. She paid me for my time this week. She's one of my regular customers. Every Tuesday and Friday I do her garden, weather permitting, then she pays me on Friday afternoon.'

'Do you come inside?'

'I usually go into the kitchen through the back door and leave the same way.'

'You don't go into the sitting room?'

'No, never. If I needed to speak to Miss Jenkins, I called for Nurse Gillespie and she called Miss Jenkins to talk to me in the kitchen, or opened the sitting room window.'

Brookland considered this for a moment. 'Thank you, Mr Miller. You can go, but please keep this conversation to yourself. We have yet to inform Mr Edward Jenkins of his aunt's death.'

'Very well. Can I tell the missus and...?' Miller asked, stopping abruptly.

'Yes, just caution her too, and anyone else.'

Miller turned to leave and paused slightly, finally deciding to head back through the front door.

Collins called after him. 'Mr Miller?' Miller froze and turned back. 'What is your shoe size?'

❖

DCI Brookland decided to visit Edward Jenkins at his office in the first instance, rather than having a constable call on him, partly as a courtesy and partly because he wanted to see the man's reactions for himself. He left DS Collins at the crime scene and had himself driven into Wringford. His driver pulled up outside of the offices of Davis and Prout, where Brookland disembarked and headed inside. A few minutes later he was shaking hands with Miss Jenkins' only relative. He seated himself in a chair close to Jenkins' desk.

'I am sorry to inform you that your aunt died last night, and I have to ask you questions in connection with that death.'

Brookland watched Jenkins' expressions change from polite interest to shock and distress. A slim, weedy man of around fifty, bespectacled, and resembling a bookstore owner or librarian, Jenkins dropped heavily into his chair.

'How - what happened, Inspector?' Jenkins asked. Brookland saw the struggle on his face, but could do little to reassure the man.

'Her death may not have been natural, I'm sorry to say. Her nurse found her dead when she arrived at the house this morning. Somebody less familiar with her habits might have assumed it was just heart failure, but Nurse Gillespie thought the circumstances suspicious and telephoned for us. It appears your aunt may have surprised a burglar beforehand. One of her displayed vases is missing, and there is evidence of a break-in.'

Jenkins slumped and stared at the floor. 'I haven't been a very good nephew to her, I'm afraid.'

Brookland watched him for a moment. 'Why is that, Mr Jenkins?' Your aunt appeared well-cared-for, and presumably comfortable in mind and body, so what leads you to believe you have been lacking?'

Jenkins looked at Brookland and said, 'I didn't visit her as often as I should. I am a partner in this firm and am kept rather busy. My wife enjoys socialising, is not— was not particularly fond of Aunt Dora, so my visits were brief and made between appointments or late in the afternoon. I relied on Nurse Gillespie and found her an excellent companion and nurse, but I should have spent more time with Aunt despite my wife's ambitions.' He frowned, thinking for a moment. 'You said there had been a theft of a vase, Chief Inspector?

'Yes, Mr Jenkins. Could you furnish me with a list of your aunt's valuables?'

'I can.' Jenkins stood up and opened a filing cabinet to the side of his desk. He withdrew a file and brought it to Brookland who opened it on his lap. It contained a short typed list. Brookland took out his notebook, made a few entries, then handed the file back to the solicitor.

'Thank you, Mr Jenkins.' Jenkins replaced the

file in the cabinet, closed it, and drew a sharp breath as Brookland continued. 'Can you tell me where you were Friday night and Saturday morning?'

He stared at Brookland and said, 'I see. I left here at six o'clock, drove home for the evening and did not leave until shortly before 10 am. I drove my wife to the hairdressers, and came here to put in an hour or so before joining her for lunch in—,' he looked at his watch, '—twenty minutes.'

'Your address?' Jenkins gave the address, and Brookland noted it, then stood up.

'Thank you, sir. You may leave for your lunch if you wish. I'll have one of my men corroborate your story with your wife later in your home. I'll have somebody inform you if there is to be an inquest, or if we need to speak to you again. Good day!

Brookland left the dazed solicitor, the office and the building at a fast pace. Once outside, he opened the car door, climbed in and was driven away in the direction of the police station.

By the time Brookland re-entered the police station in Wringford, it was well past lunchtime and into mid-afternoon. A cup of tea and a ham sandwich later, Brookland walked down the back corridor and into the small CID incident room to see DS Collins and DC Dale assembling information on the table and producing lists.

'Have we heard from the pathologist yet?' Brookland addressed himself to Collins, who looked up from his work at the table.

'Yes. He says the victim was smothered, so not heart failure after all. He'll send the report over when he's completed his post mortem.'

Brookland nodded. 'What about the area outside the pantry window?'

'There are marks in the soil, so somebody could have stood there, and there's a tree that would give easy access if someone were fit enough to swing themselves up. There's a piece of bark used to re-close the sash window, making it look secure until you see the inside fastener isn't working. From the marks on the tree, it looks like a foot was wedged to climb it.'

'That probably eliminates John Miller as a suspect,' said Brookland. ' I don't see him as the Tarzan type.'

Collins smirked. 'Not really. He did know quite a lot about Miss Jenkins' dining service and gold spoons, though.'

'Probably saw them when they were in the kitchen, being washed. He'd see most of the domestic routine from that vantage point.' Brookland surmised. 'Speaking of eliminating suspects, do we have any confirmed alibis yet?'

'Nurse is in the clear, at home with parents just as she told me. A neighbour heard a car, saw her dropped off at home by her man friend. Miller was in the local, as he said. Several witnesses saw his wife fetch him and take him home, slightly drunk. She got him to bed. Woke him up at eight-thirty, just as he said. As for Mr Edward Jenkins?'

Brookland took his cue. 'You are sending a constable to speak to Mrs Jenkins to confirm her husband's alibi. He says he left work at six o'clock on Friday evening, drove home and did not leave until shortly before 10 am Saturday morning. Here's his home address if you haven't got it.' He showed Collins his notes from earlier, and Collins copied down the address.

'Oh, and something else I wanted to speak to you about. Did you notice John Miller's abrupt halt mid-sentence after he asked if he could tell his wife what happened? He seemed to be on the point of mentioning somebody else too. And he flinched when you called him back to ask about his shoe size.'

'I did, said Collins, smiling. 'I spoke to them both, later, at their house.' He waved at his notes. Brookland took a pace nearer and picked up the sheets.

'What's this about John Miller's son, Peter?' Brookland looked at Collins' notes on the table. 'Does he have a connection to the old lady?'

'He's unaccounted for, according to his parents. Went to the pictures with friends Friday evening, apparently, but where he is now, they don't know.

He didn't come home last night and hasn't shown up this morning. I got the name of two of the friends so I've sent a constable to check on them both. Young Miller got in with the wrong crowd a few years back and was arrested for theft. He's about the right height and build to use the pantry window, but his disappearance is the main reason I've decided to add him to the suspect list.'

'What made you think of him - oh, no, let me guess. Nurse Gillespie mentioned him.'

Collins looked sheepish. 'She did. To be fair, she also mentioned the milkman, the baker and the lad who delivers from the butchers.'

Brookland laughed. 'Well, you'd better hope she doesn't fancy a job as a WPC. She might just solve your case for you! Have you ascertained alibis for those gentlemen?'

Collins flinched. 'Do you really think...?'

'No, but it's a good idea all the same. Get a couple of constables to follow up with the delivery people on Monday. What about the man friend? She said he picked her up from Miss Jenkins' house. Do we have his address?'

'Dale?' The constable had stopped what he was doing and was staring into space.

'Sorry, sir,' Dale started suddenly. 'I just remembered something. I spoke to the neighbours on each side of Miss Jenkins' house. One of them, a Mrs Beasley, said she saw John Miller digging a large hole on Friday afternoon. She wondered what it was for, but the hole was filled in again when she looked on Saturday morning.'

'Was it, indeed?' queried Brookland. 'Then I think we should send a constable over to dig it up again.'

CHAPTER TWO

"Elderly ballet star found dead at home

Shock discovery of burglary

by *Wringford Gazette and Echo* reporter

Residents of Lower Broadwood were shocked to learn yesterday of the death of Dora Jenkins, 82, former dancer with the Royal Ballet. Miss Jenkins was found dead in her sitting room, apparently of heart failure, following a burglary at her home. Police have been making enquiries among her neighbours and family, but have given no further details about their investigations. Miss Jenkins was a generous contributor to local charities, and will be much missed by all who knew her.

Dora Jenkins was born in Sussex in 1871 and had ambitions to become a ballerina from early childhood. Those ambitions were realised at the age of..."

- Wringford Gazette and Echo

❖

The next day being a Sunday, there was little reason for Brookland to spend it at the station.

Collins had informed him the previous evening that the constable who had been despatched to dig up the patch of Miss Jenkins' garden previously dug up by John Miller had found it had been refilled with soil, there being nothing buried within. On his own initiative he had swapped jobs with his colleague and sent himself to interview the Millers, his colleague now checking on Mr and Mrs Edward Jenkins' alibi, while a third was making calls to another county. Collins was in charge and would inform Brookland if anything required his attention before Monday. Brookland lingered over his breakfast and the Sunday paper, frowning at the small article halfway down the front page. Headquarters had issued a short, slightly disingenuous statement on Saturday to the effect that the elderly lady was deceased, and that cause of death was as yet undetermined; the police having been called as there had been a theft. There had been no mention of enquiries, and although that was to be expected, it had suggested something akin to knowledge of procedure. He made a mental note to check on Monday. Perhaps one of his men had let something slip, or a neighbour had spoken to a reporter. He'd make sure to remind the men about discussing the case in public. Brookland turned the page and settled back to read.

Back at the station, Collins was adding his constables' latest intelligence to his growing pile of reports. He had notes on the behaviour of the people associating with the Jenkins household from neighbours and relatives; he would have to wait until Monday before some could be contacted, but a few of the tradesmen had alibis which were quickly verified. He began to organise his notes in chronological order, annotating and cross-referencing as he went. He transferred his notes to a large sheet of paper pinned to a board, occasionally speaking to Dale for confirmation. As ideas occurred to him, he jotted them down on a separate sheet. At the end of the morning, he had a sketchy timeline and had eliminated several possible suspects, although he had few doubts about them in the first place. Eve Gillespie was never really suspected as she had drawn attention to the old lady's behaviour being at odds with a natural cause of death. John Miller could have come and gone without drawing suspicion or needing to climb through a window which he could not have done, anyway. Edward Jenkins could have found an excuse to remove the vase on a previous occasion, so it was unlikely he had chosen to steal it overnight, but he might have a motive for eliminating his aunt, so his alibi would still need to be checked.

'Dale? Has Mrs Jenkins verified her husband was at home Friday night?'

'Yes Sarge. It took several efforts, though - Mrs Jenkins was out all evening at some charitable event, although when Constable Bowers went to speak to her this morning, he overheard part of an argument between her and her husband. It appears Mrs Jenkins was having a cosy drink with one of the town councillors for part of the evening and got in late Saturday evening. However, she did verify that her husband was home and in bed Friday night.'

'Good. That rules him out, then. We have any word on young Peter Miller?'

Before Constable Dale could answer, another constable appeared at the door in motorcycle gear.

'Yes, Stevens?'

'I've spoken to two of Peter Miller's friends who say they were with him at the pictures Friday night. They parted at 10.15 pm, haven't seen him since. He was due to meet them at a coffee shop at 11.am on Saturday morning but didn't show.'

'And no word from his parents?'

'No, Sarge. Want me to ride over there and find out if he's shown up?

Collins looked at the man, and realised he'd been out all morning.

'No, take your break. Constable Dale can take the car.'

Dale nodded and was about to ask a question when a commotion in the hall made Collins rise and head out of the door, Dale and Stevens behind him. Heading for the source of the noise, he saw the desk Sergeant in a loud exchange with a young man who bore a resemblance to John Miller.

'Mr Peter Miller?'

The young man turned to face Collins. 'Yes, that's me. I heard you wanted to talk to me. Well, here I am.'

'This chap said—,' the Sergeant began.

'Yes, Sergeant,' Collins shut off the belligerent officer before he could further antagonise his visitor. 'We asked Mr Miller to present himself and he has done so. This way, Mr Miller, if you please.'

❖

'Mr Miller, we need to speak with you in connection with the death of Miss Dora Jenkins on Friday night.'

Collins sat across from a slim, dark-haired youth in a white shirt, jeans and a black leather jacket. Miller frowned. 'I don't understand. My father said Miss Jenkins died of heart failure.'

'The coroner has confirmed she was killed during a robbery.'

Miller's face dropped in consternation. 'I had nothing to do with any robbery! I was at the pictures! You can ask my friends! I would never hurt the old lady!'

'We spoke to your friends. You left them at 10.15 on Friday evening. You were to meet on Saturday morning. You failed to do so. You are acquainted with the victim, have a prior conviction for theft, have no alibi for the time of death and...

other reasons.'

Miller stared at Collins. 'Theft? I borrowed a policeman's bicycle when I was 18. It was a prank! I left it for him at the station! He was my friend's older brother! He didn't want to press charges, but his Guv'nor forced him to record it.'

Dale, who had been silently standing against the wall behind Collins, tried to hide a snigger and coughed. Collins turned around in his seat and glared at him. Dale clamped his jaws together, but caught the Miller's eye and gave a half-smile of sympathy. Collins narrowed his eyes.

'Constable? Is that true?'

'Yes, Sergeant.' Dale consulted his notes. 'Misappropriation of constabulary property, specifically one bicycle, for three hours. A witness reported it, so it was recorded.'

Collins relaxed his posture a little and continued. 'So where were you after you left the cinema, Mr Miller?'

'I met a friend who asked me for a favour.'

'And that favour was...?'

'The loan of my motorcycle to get to work early that morning. His car's engine was misfiring and had cut out suddenly. I told him it was probably just dirt in the carburettor and I'd take a look at it for him, but he said he knew a mechanic who'd look at it over the weekend.'

'So why didn't you go home? You must have

known your parents would worry.'

'I stayed at his place. I thought they knew where I was. I gave him a note. My friend said he'd call and drop it off on his way to work. It was only after I got home yesterday that I found out he hadn't called at all. Or brought my motorcycle back. I had to take the bus home, and when I came through the door, I knew I was in trouble with my parents. My father was furious. He lectured me about being inconsiderate, worrying them, losing my motorcycle, on top of being questioned about the death of Miss Jenkins by one person after another. Everything he could think of he called me out for. Then he told me to stay in my room. He forgot until this morning that he hadn't let you know I'd returned, so once he did, he told me to come straight here and report in.'

Collins nodded. 'That explains why nobody told us you were home. What is the name of this friend?'

'Hamish MacDonald.'

'He was at home all night? You didn't ask him where your motorcycle was?'

Miller hesitated and shifted in his seat. 'I don't actually know. I didn't see him again.'

'And why is that?' Collins asked, fixing the young man with a stare.'

'Because...' Miller trailed off.' Don't tell my parents, but I was in his flat... with a girl.'

Collins and Dale both drew in a sharp breath.

❖

Around the time that Peter Miller arrived at the station, Collins had Brookland informed by telephone of the man's reappearance. By the time Brookland arrived at the station, Miller was being questioned in the interview room, but he caught the last five minutes of the exchange and, from the man's demeanour, was disposed to believe in his innocence, at least as far as Miss Jenkins' murder was concerned. He opened the interview room door and Collins stood. Dale moved to swap places with Brookland. Miller looked worried, but Brookland smiled and introduced himself.

'Mr Miller. I am Detective Chief Inspector Brookland. I wish to speak to you, but I need to confer with my men for a moment. Please excuse us.'

'Of course, Chief Inspector,' said Miller, looking no less unhappy.

Once outside in the corridor, Brookland lowered his voice and said to Collins, 'I missed most of that conversation. Would you tell me what he said?'

Collins briefly summarised Miller's explanation, and Brookland nodded at the end. 'Are you satisfied he's not our killer?'

'Personally, I am inclined to believe him, but we'll need to check his story. Dale?'

'I'll get the address of the flat, and the name of the girl, if he'll give it. I'll get a constable to check on this MacDonald chap too.'

'Good, said Brookland. 'Get the registration and make of Miller's motorcycle as well. Put out a flash and see if it turns up anywhere. Also, get someone to ask Miss Gillespie if she could spare us some time for a conversation and send a car to fetch her if she's free. Ask WPC Harris to look after her until we're done with Miller.'

'Yes, sir, Sarge.' Dale nodded to both men and made brief notes in his pocketbook. Then he turned and walked back into the interview room, leaving the two men alone.

'So,' said Brookland, 'If Miller is telling the truth, this pal of his borrowed his motorcycle because his car was unavailable.'

'Or perhaps the motorcycle could use a track that a car couldn't.' Collins added.

'True,' said Brookland, or he might have chosen it because his own vehicle would be recognised.'

'Miller said that MacDonald told him his vehicle was being repaired. Perhaps he'd crashed it.'

'Assuming he actually had a car. Bob, we can speculate all we want, but until we know what he was up to, we don't know if he was simply doing a mutual favour for a friend or using him to cover up something shady.'

The door opened suddenly and Dale re-emerged

with his notebook in his hand. 'I have the address of this man MacDonald and the girl's name and number. He wasn't happy about that, but realised how suspicious it all sounded. I have the registration number of his motorcycle, but MacDonald was apparently on foot, and Miller didn't see a car so can't tell us the make and model.'

'Right,' said Brookland. 'Carry on.'

Brookland opened the interview room door and Collins followed him. Miller looked up hopefully as Brookland sat down opposite him.

'Mr Miller, thank you for co-operating with us. For reasons which I cannot confide, we were under the impression that your disappearance might be connected to Miss Jenkins' death. My men will be verifying your information, and I have given instructions for a message to be sent out to all police vehicles and stations for any sightings of your motorcycle. We need to speak to your lady friend, but if she confirms your story, we will not inform your parents or hers. That is as far as it needs to go. Is there anything else you can tell us about your wayward pal? What is his age, appearance, occupation?'

Miller had visibly relaxed after Brookland's words, and said, 'He's a few years older than me, average height and build. We knew each other as boys, moved away, then one day I went into a pub and there he was. We talked about the past, things we'd done, school, that sort of thing. He said he was working part-time at several jobs, some driving for a saleroom, some portering at a hospital, that sort of thing. That was over a year ago. I helped him move some boxes a couple of times, furniture, things like that. Didn't keep in touch after that. Then I met this girl.'

Miller stumbled over the next part and swallowed before speaking. 'We got, er, friendly, but we both live at home so we couldn't do much more than kiss in the pictures, and I only have a motorcycle so...' He paused and swallowed, 'I sort of mentioned to Hamish that we had nowhere to go and he said we could use his place for the night if I loaned him my motorcycle to get to work. He said he needed to get to his night shift at the hospital. It seemed perfect: my girl was supposed to be staying over at a friends' home after a night out.' He slumped and stared at the floor. 'When we woke up in the morning it was nearly ten, he hadn't returned and my motorcycle was nowhere to be seen. We caught the bus, and I walked her back to her home. Then I went back to see if he'd shown up yet. I made myself something to eat and waited. When I eventually got home, I got it in the neck from my parents. I told them part of the story, then found out Hamish hadn't told them I was staying at his place after all. My father made me come here to report my motorcycle stolen.'

Brookland looked at Collins, then back at Miller. He felt some sympathy for the young man and asked, 'Your pal MacDonald gave you a key to his place.'

Miller rummaged in his jeans pocket and produced a house key. Brookland took it, held it as if he hoped to learn something from its weight before handing it to Collins. 'Thank you, Mr Miller. Please give my colleague the address of this flat, your girlfriend's details and allow us to take your fingerprints for comparison should we need it. After that you can go, but please inform us if either your friend or your motorcycle turn up again. Or your friend's car, for that matter.' Then he rose and opened the door. Collins rose too. Miller got to his feet and followed Collins out of the door.

He turned at the last minute and said. 'I truly am sorry about Miss Jenkins. She was a very kind lady, and she didn't deserve to go like that.'

Miller had scarcely left the station when a police car drove up. The outside door opened and WPC Harris walked in, followed by Eve Gillespie. The two were talking quietly together when Brookland and Collins walked up to them.

'Good evening, Nurse Gillespie,' said Brookland. Collins added his greeting. 'Sorry to ask you in on a Sunday, but we have some questions that we hope you can answer.'

'Of course, Chief Inspector, Sergeant.' she nodded to each in turn. 'How can I help?'

Brookland opened the door to his office and indicated for Eve to enter. She took the seat in front of Brookland's desk as he took his own seat. He drew a sheet of paper towards him, uncapped his pen and looked up.

'Miss Gillespie,' Brookland began, 'a neighbour recalled seeing John Miller digging a large hole in the back garden on Friday afternoon. Do you know about this?'

'Indeed, I do. Miss Jenkins asked him to divide a large clump of iris and plant half of it elsewhere. He dug the hole in preparation, but then Miss Jenkins changed her mind and decided to offer it to a friend instead. He must have filled in the hole before he left that day.'

'Well, that explains that,' said Collins, who had taken up a position in front of the window near to Brookland's desk.

'You thought the stolen vase might be buried there?' Eve asked.

'It was a possibility, albeit a remote one. A neighbour noticed the hole being dug and told one of my officers.'

'Mrs Beasley, I imagine.' Eve smiled.

Brookland nodded. 'Yes. We didn't expect to find anything there, and indeed we didn't. It's seldom that easy, but occasionally thieves do stupid things. However, I do need to ask you about Mr Bracewell, as according to Mrs Beasley, he has been inside Miss Jenkins' house too.'

Eve frowned. 'You think James is involved? Why?'

Brookland paused for a moment. 'We have to follow every possible lead, Nurse Gillespie, even if it is just to eliminate people from our enquiries. As we have with you.' He smiled and continued. 'So, could you tell me the name of the public house you visited on Friday evening?'

'The Crown in Lower Broadwood, Chief Inspector.'

'And Mr Bracewell is a journalist? Which newspaper does he work for?'

'The *Wringford Gazette and Echo*.'

'Does he work away?'

'Yes, sometimes. He goes where he's sent to cover events within the county.'

'Do you know his home address?'

'No, Chief Inspector. I know he lives in Wringford, and I have his work telephone number.' Eve opened her bag and removed a slip of paper from her purse. She handed it to Brookland, who copied it and handed it back. She returned it to its original location and closed her bag.

'Anything else, Chief Inspector?'

'A description of him, please. Unless you have a photograph?'

Eve smiled and reopened her bag. She produced a small black-and-white image of herself with a slim, good-looking, smiling man in his early twenties. He was dressed smartly and leaned against a railing.

'We met in a cafe near the *Gazette* office in December. One of the paper's photographers took that when he spotted us talking one day.'

'I'll see it's returned to you, Miss. Thank you for your help today. I'll get a constable to drive you home.'

After Eve had left the station, Brookland walked into the incident room and handed Collins the photograph and his notes.

'This is James Bracewell. He looks slim enough to climb through the pantry window. Miss Gillespie doesn't know his address, but here's the number for his newspaper. Find out if they have his address on file, and when he's next due at work.

Collins nodded and said, 'I've got a constable checking with the Criminal Records Office at Scotland Yard to see if MacDonald has any previous convictions, and I've had a flash put out on Miller's motorcycle. I've sent two constables to Mac-Donald's flat to search it and ask the other tenants and the landlord if they saw him come home, and when he left again.'

'Right. I'll see you tomorrow. Good night.'

'Good night, sir.' Collins watched his superior walk out of the station before he himself headed back into the incident room.

❖

"Suspicious death in Lower Broadwood

Police search for burglar

by *Wringford Gazette and Echo* reporter

Police are treating the death of Dora Jenkins, aged 82, a former ballerina with the Royal Ballet, as suspicious. Miss Jenkins, of Lower Broadwood, was found dressed in her nightclothes in her sitting room on Saturday morning. It is thought she surprised a burglar late Friday night or early Saturday morning. The police are pursuing several lines of enquiry which they hope will lead to an early arrest."

- Wringford Gazette and Echo

❖

When Brookland arrived at the station the following day, it was a little after ten-thirty. He'd taken a detour to speak to the Detective Chief Superintendent about the case and was looking forward to a cup of tea. The station was busy with the sound of telephones and typewriters. Not wishing to disturb those working, Brookland caught WPC Harris' eye, made a 'T' sign and raised an eyebrow in request. Louise smiled and nodded, pointing to a box of biscuits on her desk. Brookland nodded again, smiled and walked to his office. Brookland had no problem making his own tea but was the first to credit WPC Harris with making a better brew than he, and he was often disposed to take advantage of that gift. In return (or was it recompense?) he gave her many of the undercover assignments, for which she'd shown both aptitude and enthusiasm. He felt a fatherly concern for the young WPC, but regulations aside, he knew she was averse to being given special consideration because of her gender. She preferred to take equal turns with the men whenever possible, and had more than once proven herself a capable and plucky officer in a tight spot.

In due course, the tea and a plate of biscuits appeared on his desk, and he thanked her and gave her a smile which she returned. DS Collins had seen his boss arrive, as well as the biscuits, and brought his own tea and a folder into the DCI's office.

'Morning, Bob. Have a biscuit and unburden yourself. What do we have?'

'Morning, sir.' Collins dropped into the spare chair and put his cup down. He helped himself to the proffered biscuit and opened the folder on his lap. 'We've searched MacDonald's flat. There were a few long dark hairs on the pillow in the bedroom, suggesting a female slept there, which fits with Miller's statement. Apart from the usual things like a few items of clothing - a torn shirt, an old tie, but no shoes. There was spare linen, towels, that sort of thing, but it was little of any help to us. There were a few receipts for clothing from Wringford shops, a notepad with local telephone numbers written on it, stationery in a drawer, a few newspapers, a magazine about cars, a few glasses and a near-empty bottle of whiskey. The lab boys have taken those but I'm not holding out much hope. There's no word on Miller's motorcycle, but it's early yet. I phoned Bracewell's newspaper yesterday; they confirmed he's a journalist. The editor, Ed Delaney, wasn't in then, so they didn't know if he's on assignment this weekend. However, he got the message and phoned me just now. Apparently, Bracewell's covering a flower show in Hawford this weekend. They have a home address for him, but it's not the one he gave us, and while they knew it was out of date, nobody had thought to get the current one from him.'

Brookland sighed. 'Oh, well, we'll have to wait for him to return from his trip, then. Anything else?'

'I've sent someone to the Crown pub when it opens, to see if Nurse Gillespie and Bracewell were seen regularly, especially on Fridays. I've also put the word out to local antique dealers in case the stolen vase turns up.'

'Check out those telephone numbers, see who they belong to and why he might have contacted them. What about MacDonald? Anything back from Records?'

'Nothing yet, sir. How was your visit to the Guv'nor?'

'The usual. Is it worth our time, manpower etc.? Are we sure it's not just a heart attack and a minor theft?

'And you said...?'

'Did he want the newspapers to criticise us for overlooking a murder and a burglary because the victim was an old lady and not a prominent, wealthy politician?'

Collins smiled. 'He must have liked that reminder,' he said. Brookland nodded, smiling.

'About as much as when he had to explain to the Detective Chief Superintendent that he'd taken men off of a search for a missing child to increase the men protecting a controversial trade-union boss.'

Collins grinned. 'Rather you than me, sir. Do you think Miller's friend will turn up with the motorcycle sometime?'

'I don't know. We only have it from Miller that MacDonald has a car, that the flat is his. It's probably rented. Did you find a cheque book, rent book, any documentation?'

'No, nothing like that. But, if Miller is correct, MacDonald has several jobs and may need transport. I'll see if we can trace the flat's landlord.' Collins rose from his seat and took the folder with him, leaving Brookland to nod to no one in particular.

❖

Meanwhile, the constable sent to verify MacDonald's movements was able to speak to a neighbour who confirmed seeing MacDonald late Friday evening, perhaps around 11.30. He had another man with him. He was seen leaving on foot at around 10 am the following morning, but the neighbour who was tending to his garden at the time could not recall hearing or seeing a motor car. However, it became moot when the neighbour admitted to slight deafness, '...a result of all those bombs going off in the war.' The constable expressed sympathy and tried another neighbour. This lady had herself been away and so could not contribute much. She thought the gentleman in question had a motor car but could not be certain as it was not parked nearby.

It was not until mid-afternoon that Collins heard from the constable he had sent to the Crown public house. His officer had shown the picture of James Bracewell and Eve Gillespie to the publican who had identified them as regular patrons in the lounge. He remembered them there last Friday. Yes, he was sure about that, because a patron at the bar had remarked that the gentleman with her looked familiar, and was that his motor car outside? The landlord had not been able to confirm this, and did not know the gentleman's name, but why not ask him? Then the gentleman in question looked up and met the eyes of the man at the bar and turned pale. Said gentleman then drank up his beer and urged the young lady to drink up her sherry as it was getting late - about 9.45 pm and of course they close at 10 pm. The two then left, and the sound of a motor car starting could be heard. The man at the bar drank his beer, and he also left. What did he look like? Thickset, strong, as if he might be a dockworker or a boxer. Where did he go next? The landlord couldn't say, as he was serving last orders prior to closing time. The constable handed back the photograph. Collins took it and thanked the constable for his efforts. The man smiled back his thanks, nodded and left. Collins added this new information to his notes and placed them and the photograph in the files in the incident room. A note from DC Dale mentioned a response to their earlier message, producing a report of Miller's motorcycle being seen on Sunday evening by a PC in another county, apparently parked in a quiet back street with no sign of damage, quite cold as if it had been there a while. The constable had called it in from the nearest police post, but on returning had found the motorcycle had gone. He had walked down nearby streets to look for it, returned to the post and updated his report. Collins was next handed a note from MacDonald's landlord, confirming the flat was rented by one Hamish MacDonald since April 1952. Rent was paid in cash fortnightly, in advance. The landlord thought MacDonald drove a car, but couldn't be sure as he'd never asked. Collins added the information to his other notes and when Brookland appeared to see what was new, Collins updated him on the latest developments.

Much later, Collins walked to Brookland's

office, knocked and entered. Brookland looked up expectantly.

'Those telephone numbers on MacDonald's notepad were to a local garage and a taxi company. They don't remember a call from anyone named MacDonald, so it's likely he never called them.'

Brookland sighed. 'I didn't really expect they'd be useful, but I did hope for something out of the ordinary. We're fast running out of leads to follow up. I hope something turns up soon.'

Collins nodded in agreement. 'I'm off now, sir.'

Brookland looked back at the report he was writing. 'I'll be leaving soon, Bob. Have a good evening.'

'You too, sir. Goodnight.'

Closing the door, he picked up his hat and coat from his own office and headed out to the front of the station, bidding his men goodnight as he left.

CHAPTER THREE

"Heart failure death now confirmed as murder
by *Wringford Gazette and Echo* reporter

Police are following new information in their investigation of the sudden death of Dora Jenkins last Friday. At first believing the death to be from natural causes, they now believe Miss Jenkins was murdered by person or persons as yet unknown. To this end, they have interviewed members of Miss Jenkins' household and neighbours, as well as local tradesmen, and are pursuing leads which they hope will assist them in identifying the criminal or criminals concerned. No new statements have been released by police since Saturday."

- *Wringford Gazette and Echo*

Tuesday morning found Brookland and Collins returning to scan new information from Monday evening. In addition to the details on Hamish Mac-Donald's flat was the second sighting of Miller's motorcycle courtesy of the constabulary in the adjacent county. From this subsequent sighting on

Monday, it appeared that MacDonald was racking up the miles that weekend. Dale had plotted the motorcycle sightings on a map, complete with tags confirming date and time. In the meantime, enquiries made at local hospitals revealed no-one by the name of Hamish MacDonald was employed as a porter or any other role at any of the hospitals within fifty miles. It was beginning to look as if MacDonald had lied about that job.

There was nothing more they could squeeze out of the facts of MacDonald's actions; they still had no clue if he had a car, if it was out of action or why he spent the weekend riding a stolen motorcycle around the next county. For all they knew, there was no link between his actions and the murder of Dora Jenkins. MacDonald may just be a man with unknown private business who didn't want to confide his plans to his former school friend. The lack of a traceable occupation seemed suspicious, but perhaps Miller had misunderstood or MacDonald wasn't the confiding type. Or perhaps he was just plain paranoid. Brookland had met a few of those in his career, but switching vehicles sounded more like the man was hoping to remain anonymous rather than behaving as if he was deranged. Brookland fervently hoped they weren't engaged on a wild goose chase after all. There was still no word from the lab either. Brookland decided to check for himself if no word came through by the end of the day.

They were beginning to run out of ideas as to what direction to take next when, mid-morning, Brookland received a telephone call.

When a constable appeared in the doorway to inform Brookland he had a call from a James Bracewell, three heads shot up from their tasks. Brookland got to his feet and moved around the messenger, heading swiftly for the telephone in his office. Collins and Dale followed him, watching from the corridor.

Brookland met their eyes as he lifted the receiver and took the call.

'Detective Chief Inspector Brookland.'

'Inspector, this is James Bracewell. My lady friend tells me you want to speak to me.'

'That I do, Mr Bracewell. As I'm sure Nurse Gillespie will have told you, we are investigating Miss Jenkins' death. Can you come down to the station to give a statement, please?'

One hour later, a slim, good-looking man in his early twenties, dressed in a suit and tie, sat smiling at Brookland and Collins in the interview room. Easy charm characterised the man before them.

'Thank you for coming here today, Mr Bracewell,' Brookland smiled pleasantly. 'If you could give us an account of last Friday, from the time you collected Nurse Gillespie from Miss Jenkins' house.'

'Certainly.' Bracewell straightened himself in his chair and began. As he spoke, Collins took down Bracewell's words in his notebook.

'I arrived just as she was leaving, I stood by the gate and greeted her. We walked to my car, and I opened the door for her. I drove us to the Crown public house; we went inside for a drink before they closed. Then I drove her back to her parents' home. I said goodnight, gave her a kiss on the cheek, waved and got back into my car. I stopped at an off-licence machine for a packet of cigarettes and went home. On Saturday, I left for an assignment at a flower show, stayed in a room for two nights and returned on Monday, dropped off my copy to my editor. I phoned Eve last night, and she told me what had happened, and that the police wanted to talk to me. And here I am.'

'Can you give me the make, model and registration number of your vehicle, please?'

Bracewell frowned slightly and gave the details. Collins again wrote in his notebook.

'And your address?' Bracewell gave the address and watched Collins writing.

'And the address where you stayed in Hawford?'

Bracewell was visibly startled. 'How did you know...? Oh, of course, my editor. For a moment there I thought you'd pulled off a magic trick or something.'

'Quite. The address?'

Bracewell gave the address of a Hawford boarding house. As before, he watched Collins write down his answers. When Brookland next looked up, Bracewell asked, 'Do you have any idea why Miss Jenkins was murdered? I gather from Eve that she surprised a burglar. She didn't mention what was stolen, or whether there were other robberies in the area, but she said some of the neighbours have been talking about it.'

Brookland thought for a moment before answering. He had assumed Eve Gillespie would have told him all she knew, but perhaps she didn't want to say anything out of turn, unprofessionally. Or perhaps it was just out of loyalty to her late employer. Something wriggled in Brookland's brain, but he couldn't place it. He decided to err on the side of caution.

'We are aware of at least one item stolen, possibly more, from one or more locations within the house. We had two suspects, both now eliminated, and we are looking into reports of prowlers in the area. We have had to interview all those we knew had some association with Miss Jenkins, no matter how slight. However, we believe there is the possibility of outside, er, parties gaining entry under false pretences and leaving no evidence to speak of. This makes things more difficult for us, of course, but you can assure Miss Gillespie that we will not rest until we have the culprit or culprits under lock and key.'

Bracewell looked reassured. 'Thank you, Chief Inspector. We both appreciate your efforts, and I understand the need to be certain of your facts.'

'Thank you, Mr Bracewell. If we need anything further from you, we will let you know. Good day.'

'Good day, Chief Inspector, Sergeant.'

Bracewell stood and walked out of the room. Collins frowned at his boss and said, 'Did I miss something? We don't have any other recent burglaries in the area.'

'No, we don't. But he doesn't know that.' Brookland smiled at his colleague's puzzlement. 'Bob, he's a journalist. I had assumed Nurse Gillespie would tell him all she knew, but evidently, she did not. I'm not sure whether she was being professional or circumspect so I thought it might be helpful to let him think we have a wider field of suspects than we in fact do.'

'You think he has a professional interest in the case?' Collins asked.

'Honestly?' Brookland stood and walked around his desk towards the door. 'I'm just hoping he's up to something because I don't trust his manner. Let's look into the information he gave us.'

'Right.' Collins said, rising to his feet.

'One more thing. Impress upon the men the need to keep the details of this case to ourselves. I don't want our investigation compromised by a careless word in the wrong ear.'

'I'm sure none of our men...' Collins began.

'And I want it to stay that way. No names or details outside of the station.' Brookland grinned suddenly. 'Tell the men to converse in code or signs or something. Mum's the word.'

Collins nodded and left Brookland alone in the room.

Now we'll see what our conniving columnist makes of that!

❖

By Tuesday evening, Collins had assembled a timeline for Bracewell's known movements. His car was familiar to Miss Jenkins' neighbours and was also seen near the Crown public house. A call to the landlady of the B&B in Hawford confirmed Bracewell had stayed there. Yes, he arrived Saturday afternoon and took breakfast Sunday and Monday mornings. No, she had not seen a motor car, but there was no private parking so could not confirm or deny its existence. Yes, Mr Bracewell had a small overnight bag with him. Yes, he had paid the bill in cash. To add to the evidence supporting Bracewell's story was the appearance in the *Wringford Gazette and Echo* of a small piece about the flower show in Hawford.

A constable had been despatched to verify the home address Bracewell had given them. He tried the doorbell, knocked and called through the letterbox but there was no response and the interior of the house was dark. Neither of the neighbours were in, and so the constable came away. Collins asked him to return the next day to try again.

A call to the registration office confirmed Bracewell's ownership of a 1937 dark green Austin Seven. Just to be thorough, Collins had Dale send requests for any sightings of that vehicle to other stations in the Wringford area on Friday or Saturday.

Dale was adding this latest information to the investigation notes when Collins walked in. 'So, we have a car belonging to one man, but nobody's seen it, a motorcycle belonging to a second man, stolen, and ridden by another who hasn't been seen, but the motorcycle has.'

'Er, yes, Sarge,' said Dale. 'No sightings of Mac-Donald since Friday evening or Miller's motorcycle since Monday.' Dale liked his facts straightforward. Collins tended to work with information until it fit together like a puzzle. He would arrange and rearrange ideas and facts in a tidy but meaningful way. Dale lacked the imagination and creativity to do this, so he prided himself on being thorough and efficient. Surprisingly, the two worked harmoniously for the most part, seldom crossing each other, with Collins extracting the detail from Dale's reports as if he were creating a story; a landscape from a few sketches or a concerto from an assortment of raw themes. Ever patient, Collins would pick at the evidence until satisfied he had the whole sequence of events. Which, as yet, he did not.

'What about MacDonald's car? Do we know what make it is?'

Dale shook his head. 'There's no record of his owning a car, so either he was lying or it's stolen.'

'Check if any vehicles have been reported stolen or found recently.'

'How recently?'

'The past month should do. Ignore anything fancy: it would be too memorable.'

Dale nodded and headed to his desk and the telephone. Collins continued to stare at the time-line, but nothing sparked any ideas. A note handed to him by a uniformed constable indicated a call from the police lab - none of the fingerprints in MacDonald's flat were helpful. Some belonged to the young couple, mostly in the bedroom and bathroom. That left seven different prints, presumably previous guests as well as MacDonald, or, in the case of the whiskey, the off-licence staff too.

Collins sighed at the news; more disappointment to add to their meagre collection of facts.

Around the middle of the afternoon, Brookland and Collins settled in the incident room to consider what they knew. Peter Miller's motorcycle was still missing, MacDonald hadn't returned to his flat, there were no cars recovered in the past week, and none reported stolen that might have been used by MacDonald. None of the fences contacted would admit to seeing the stolen vase, although there was little chance that they would admit to it if they had.

Brookland swallowed down the last of his tea and put the cup down 'All right. The footprints underneath the pantry window were too badly scuffed to be of use, beyond indicating that the owner was of middle height and weight. Entry through the window indicates a slightly built man, not unfit and probably under forty years old. No vehicle was seen at that time, let alone the culprit. All our suspects have alibis. Now we need new ones. Who have we overlooked?

Collins shook his head. 'I admit I'm stumped. The old lady had few visitors; none likely to climb in through that pantry window, yet somebody did. Did they know what they were looking for, or was it just opportune? Our regular lags don't attack the owners, they wait for them to go away. It has to be a non-professional job.'

'Unless it's a pair of amateurs.' Brookland theorised.

'How do you mean?' asked Collins, puzzled.

Brookland stood and said, 'Suppose we have one opportunistic burglar, and one clumsy amateur, working together or separately. Burglar A climbs in through the window, looking for something in particular. Burglar B follows and hides. Burglar A disturbs the old lady and kills her, B follows A back to his car, knocks him out, dumps the unconscious body... and makes off with the car and vase! No, that's just the stuff of fiction. I give up. Did we get a value on that stolen vase?'

'Around £600, I believe.'

'Then either it was specifically stolen for some reason, or it'll need to be fenced in London or other sizeable city. You heard nothing locally, I believe?'

'No,' said Collins. 'I rather doubted we would.'

'No. But that doesn't mean it hasn't gone else-where, to a buyer, or an auction house.'

Collins frowned hard and then got up to search through his notes on the table. 'What is it, Bob?' asked Brookland.

'I remembered something Peter Miller said. Here.' He handed Brookland his notebook. 'Peter Miller said MacDonald had told him where he worked: "He said he was working part-time at several jobs, some driving for a saleroom, some portering at a hospital. We know the latter isn't true, what about the former?"

'Driving for a saleroom. You think he's savvy enough to steal a valuable vase? How would he know where to lay his hands on it? Oh, I see.' said Brookland. 'You think somebody else stole it, and MacDonald recognised its value and stole it him-self?'

'Well, you did mention the two-burglar theory first. Perhaps he knows where to fence it. Perhaps that's where he's gone.'

'That still doesn't tell us who stole it in the first place, but if we can find the saleroom, they might give us more on this MacDonald bloke.'

'I'll get someone on it right away.' Collins left the room to find one of his men and met Dale in the corridor.

❖

'Ah, Sarge, I just got a telephone call from a PC Gareth Melrose at Trent Street Station. Apparently, he just heard about our check on Bracewell's car. He was chasing a burglar he'd just interrupted in the process of picking the lock on a local jeweller's shop. The bloke he was chasing threw away his pick-locks as he ran past a dark Austin Seven. PC Melrose thinks it was the same registration plate.'

'Friday night? Are you sure? What time?'

Collins had opened his mouth to speak, but Brookland, who had just appeared in the doorway behind Collins, spoke first.

'PC Melrose isn't entirely sure, but he thinks it was around 10:30 pm.'

'Thank you, Dale. Did he file a 'vehicles seen' slip?

'Yes, sir, but the car lights were on, and he only got a glimpse of the registration number in passing. He had a busy night, and the car was gone by the time he passed that way again, nearer to 2 am. However, when he heard we were asking he called it in.'

'Good. Let's have that slip. And ask PC Melrose in for a short statement when he can?'

'Already in hand, sir,' replied Dale.

Brookland nodded and returned to the files he and Collins had been perusing. Collins apprised Dale of the conversation about MacDonald's possible employment and gave the constable his instructions to have someone telephone the salerooms around the Wringford area.

Collins rejoined Brookland as he added the new details. 'Sounds as if Bracewell was truthful. He said he stopped for cigarettes before going home.'

'Yes, he did. The trip to Hawford checks out, so perhaps MacDonald is our man. Let me know what Dale finds out, Bob. I have some reports to get to.'

'Yes, sir.' Collins stepped aside as Brookland headed back to his office. Collins issued a few follow-up requests to the remaining officers, then he too left for the evening.

By a quarter to six, Dale and two constables had spoken to all the auction rooms listed in the local telephone directory, plus a few private antique specialists. They were conferring as to where to look next when the final number turned out to be the correct one. Yes, they had employed a young, part-time driver, and confirmed the name was Hamish MacDonald. However, due to a downturn in business they had not employed him in the last few weeks. Yes, they had a contact number for him; on checking, Dale saw that it matched the house where MacDonald rented his flat.

Brookland had spent the last few hours catching up on paperwork unrelated to their investigation. He picked up the latest information from Dale and his colleagues before leaving the station. Collins issued a few follow-up requests to the remaining officers, then he too left for the evening. Dale found himself a cup of tea and a comfortable chair. He spread the information sheets across the table in front of him, picked up his notebook and began to write. After a quarter of an hour, he sat back in his chair and reassessed what he'd written.

James Bracewell - *address in Wringford* - *in Hawford for two nights on business* - *returned, assignment completed as confirmed by the printer at the Gazette. Car identified and number checked. Probably in use to and from the pub, possibly seen in town at 10:30 pm Friday, as per his statement. Presumably drove to Hawford but nobody saw the car there.*

Hamish MacDonald - *address in Wringford, no sign of occupant* - *no car registered, though he told Miller it was out of order* - *borrowed Miller's motorcycle, spent the weekend in the next county. Reason unknown. Where did he stay, and why?*

Questions - *if Hamish stole a motorcycle, did he*

also steal a car? Check reports of stolen cars - how did he usually get to work? Where did he work, if not at a hospital or auction room? Perhaps enquire at the labour exchange? He added these questions to his checklist.

No information received back from other counties. Must chase CRO tomorrow.

Dale stared at his notes for many minutes, hoping for more inspiration when a loud booming voice behind him made him jump.

'Go home, lad! You're not on overtime!' the bluff duty sergeant barked from the door.

Dale scrambled to his feet. 'No, Skipper, I've just finished. Goodnight!' He bolted from the room before the sergeant could say another word.

CHAPTER FOUR

"Police seek motorcycle rider in murder case

by *Wringford Gazette and Echo* reporter

'Police believe they have important leads in the murder of Dora Jenkins of Lower Broadwood, which occurred last Friday. They have been showing sketches of a person they wish to interview to potential witnesses in the local area. This person is believed to travel around by motorcycle, although police have not explained the connection to the murder, and no details about a new suspect have been released."

- Wringford Gazette and Echo

Brookland and Collins leaned over the table in the incident room. Dale's files were spread before them, and the map with the trail showing sightings of Miller's motorcycle was placed above them.

'So, we have two sightings, Sunday and Monday, at some distance from here. Then nothing.' Collins said.

Brookland nodded. 'The motorcycle was out in the open, then hidden in a garage or shed, or just somewhere unobserved. But what was the rider doing?'

'Visiting fences? Auction houses? We still don't know if he is our suspect,' said Collins thoughtfully. 'He may have some other part to play in all this, may not be the murderer at all. On some errand, looking for someone or something.'

Brookland nodded again. 'He needed young Miller's motorcycle for the weekend, and not for work. He could have caught the bus for that. They run late. Plus, he didn't go home: he left the county, apparently.' He waved his hand over the map. 'He's up to something, but what? There's been no sign of him at his flat?'

'Apparently not. I had a constable check yesterday evening. No MacDonald, no motorcycle.'

'And if he hasn't been seen since Monday, has he moved to another county, or returned home? Is the motorcycle hidden in a garage or shed until it's needed, or has it been sold on?'

Collins shook his head. 'We have a lot of unanswered questions but until we get...'

'We must be overlooking something,' interrupted Brookland impatiently. 'Everybody appears to have an alibi, nobody could have killed the old lady, yet apparently, somebody did. Nobody has a motive for the theft, yet somebody must have broken in for that exact purpose. And we have a missing man who appears to have no connection to the murder, but borrowed an old friend's motorcycle, apparently doing him a return favour, and inadvertently making him a suspect, except that he has an alibi. Is it just coincidence that Miller and MacDonald knew each other well enough to trade favours, and Miller knew the victim? MacDonald doesn't have a record, but does he have a relative we can trace?'

Collins got up and walked to the door, meeting a constable arriving from the corridor.

'What is it, Stevens?'

'Telephone call, Sarge. Peter Miller says he's found his motorcycle.'

❖

Mid-afternoon on Wednesday brought two pieces of useful information. The call from Peter Miller to say he'd walked out of his workplace at a local garage midday to find his motorcycle parked a few yards away, muddy tank almost empty but the motorcycle apparently none the worse for its adventure. He had run back into the garage to make a phone call to the station while one of his colleagues watched over the newly-recovered machine. A call was made to have the lab fingerprint it in situ; a small crowd of mechanics and passers-by watching quietly a few feet away. Then Miller was allowed to move it into the garage for safety. By the time he appeared at the police station the motorcycle, a 1947 Ariel Square 4, was clean and presentable. It had, of course, been wiped clean of fingerprints, as the fingerprint expert called in to dust it earlier had not found a single one: not even its owner's.

The second piece of news was that MacDonald's flat was now leased to a new tenant, as MacDonald had apparently arranged for a friend to take over the lease a week after his disappearance. Collins had taken the telephone call from MacDonald's landlord; having requested of that gentleman that he would inform them of anything pertaining to MacDonald or the flat, said gentleman duly rang the station and asked for Detective Sergeant Collins by name. After a brief exchange of information, Collins returned to the incident room and added his notes to the investigation.

Brookland followed him in with a teacup and saucer in each hand, passing one to Collins with a comment. 'From the look on your face, that wasn't a helpful call.'

Collins shrugged. 'Not really. MacDonald's landlord says MacDonald has resigned his lease, requesting it be transferred to another tenant in the building. The landlord already rents to the other tenant and wanted to make repairs to his flat, so he agreed. MacDonald has sidestepped us.'

'It's clear he expects someone to be looking for him,' said Brookland, 'but for what reason? He borrows a friend's motorcycle, with his permission, but retains it longer than expected. That would put him in Miller's bad books, but why clear out of your flat? That looks like he wants to hide from someone. Is it us or someone else?'

'He's raced around the countryside for two days, evidently looking for someone or something, yet nobody can explain why.' Collins added. 'Blackmail, threat or panic? And where is he living now?'

'We don't know if this is related to our murder case, or simply coincidence that Peter Miller has someone in his past who's probably up to no good.' Brookland drained his tea and put the china down firmly, rattling the cup. 'This could be a complete waste of time. We really do need to know if they are connected. We could be chasing this man for nothing.'

Collins noted his superior's agitation and nodded. 'I agree, but we have no other suspects, or at least, none without alibis. I did ask Dale to check further into MacDonald.' He got up and went to look for Dale, leaving Brookland scowling at nobody.

❖

Collins found Dale just as he was putting the receiver down. Dale looked up and grinned at his sergeant.

'Please tell me you have something good,' Collins said, hopefully. Dale rose and drew himself up.

'I have, Sarge.'

'Then come and tell it to the Inspector and me. We could do with something hopeful.'

They walked back to Brookland, who looked at Dale's cheerful expression and said, 'Constable Dale, do you have something to cheer up your disillusioned superiors?'

'Yes, sir. Hamish MacDonald has a father who was recently in prison for receiving stolen goods.'

Brookland's jaw dropped. Collins sat down in his chair, glanced at the timeline, and back at Brookland. 'It could fit. Where was this father...?'

'Joseph. Joey.'

Brookland raised an amused eyebrow.

'Where was he staying at Her Majesty's pleasure?' Collins asked, smiling slightly.

'Er, Lewes, Sarge.' Dale paused.

'Go on, Constable,' said Brookland, encouragingly.

'Yes, sir. It appears that this Joey MacDonald, Hamish' father, was in prison when his wife died, leaving young Hamish alone in the world at age 12, apart from a grandmother known to be living somewhere in France. Hamish was put into a children's home and subsequently adopted since Joey was in and out of prison for years. His last address is in Brighton. No known address for Hamish once he was adopted.'

'Sentences?'

'Mostly receiving stolen goods, the last sentence being 2 years. Quiet, orderly and well-behaved in prison, so released early, after only twenty months. Now aged 46.'

'Do we have an address for him?' asked Collins.

'Not as yet. I have asked the East Sussex police to call me back when they have any more information.'

'When was he released?' asked Brookland.

'Last week. He gave a friend's address, but the friend hasn't seen him. Oh, and one more thing. Somebody else has been asking after him since his release. Said he was a prison officer, name of Wright.'

'Hamish looking for his father, perhaps.' Collins said. 'Perhaps that's who he was looking for. He could very well be our burglar.'

Brookland nodded. 'We really do need to find out what he looks like. Dale, get young Miller to give a description to our sketch artist as soon as possible. See if he'll come after work today.'

'Right, sir.' Dale took himself back to his telephone once more.

'Realistically, we have nothing. Even if we know what he looks like, we still don't know how he's connected to our case,' Brookland said quietly. 'We are guessing that he's got the vase simply because he's related to a known fence, and because he went missing after borrowing a friend's motorcycle.'

'And moved without a trace,' said Collins. He was rapidly feeling depressed and frustrated at their inability to move the case forward. Brookland couldn't help but notice his Sergeant's morale had dipped; he was only too well aware that they had little in the way of evidence, suspects or witnesses after four days' efforts.

'Go home, Bob. Fresh start in the morning.'

Collins shook his head. 'I want to see that sketch first.'

'We may not get it today. You might as well_' Brookland stopped abruptly as Dale appeared in the doorway.

'Sir, Peter Miller agreed. He'll come here directly after work.'

❖

At 6.30 that evening, Peter Miller showed up as promised. A constable had visited the garage where Miller worked, requesting his presence at the police station in connection with the theft of his motorcycle. The constable had been forewarned and had confined himself to the event in front of Miller's colleagues without reference to the circumstances behind it. Miller had been grateful for the circumspection; Collins had no need of revealing Miller's indiscretion; his embarrassment was enough to make him cooperate. He told the police artist what he could recall of Mac-Donald's appearance and left when Collins was satisfied with the result.

Collins showed the sketch to Brookland, who looked at it for half a minute and sighed. The sketch was of a pleasant-looking young man, but lacking any detail that might be useful in identification.

'Oh, well, I suppose I had my hopes up too high. This could be anyone. Perhaps if we get a constable to show this down at the auction room, somebody might confirm it looks something like MacDonald?'

'Worth a try, I suppose.' Collins moved to the door, but Brookland called him back.

'Bob, get the constable to take the sketch artist along if she'll come. Somebody else might have a better memory for detail.'

'Right.' Collins left Brookland alone in the room. Picking up the details on McDonald Senior, Brookland pondered the son's behaviour, drawing his notepad nearer to write out the points as he thought of them.

1. Hamish MacDonald hadn't gone near his father since his incarceration, yet after a decade, he suddenly goes looking for him. Definitely not paternal affection, thought Brookland, so:

2. It must be because of his knowledge and contacts.

3. That suggests something illegal, and we know he's keeping a low profile.

4. His father fences stolen goods - MacDonald may

have the stolen vase.

5. He can't be a professional thief, though, because he'd know where to go...

A voice over his shoulder made Brookland start.

'6. He gave up his flat this week.' Collins added. 'Sorry, sir, didn't mean to startle you, but you didn't respond when I spoke the first time, so I was curious as to what had you so absorbed.'

'Just writing my thoughts down on paper. What was it I didn't hear you say?'

'Constable Stevens is taking Miss Peters, our artist, to the auction room first thing tomorrow morning. Along with her previous sketch from Miller's description.'

'Good. Though I'm not sure where we go from here, even if the sketch is better. Hamish doesn't have a record; we knew that already. We really need to know what he's up to.'

Collins sighed and sat down heavily. Despite the progress they'd made discovering a possible connection to the murder, Collins was still deflated. There were substantial pieces that were missing, including the most crucial of all: the identity of the murderer.

'Yes, we certainly do,' Collins said after a moment. 'We have nothing to tell us where he fits into the investigation, or if he fits into it at all.

We don't know if we have a missing murderer, a missing thief and murderer, a missing thief or just a missing man. We have no evidence to point to our culprit or culprits, nobody saw anything suspicious, and apart from the detention of a motorcycle beyond the expected twelve-hour period, nothing to follow up. We don't know if Mac-Donald meeting Miller is coincidence or planned. I'm inclined to believe Miller; he told us the one thing that made him look suspicious, and it actually pointed away from him as a suspect. We have nothing else left to us.'

'All we have is a man behaving oddly, and that may simply be because we don't know the circumstances behind that behaviour.' Brookland added. 'We have no other loose ends to investigate at present, and I don't think MacDonald is an innocent law-abiding citizen going about his business. If he were, he wouldn't have given Miller those half-truths about his job and why he needed the motorcycle. He had no reason not to be forthright with a pal, especially when Miller's own behaviour was devious at best. Yet he lied about work and communicating with Miller Senior. I'll bet this week's salary he's doing something shady.'

'I won't take that bet,' Collins said ruefully, 'and I doubt anyone in the station will, but there are a number of bets on who the culprit is and where MacDonald went.'

Brookland raised an eyebrow interrogatively.

'Some of the lads feel we haven't exhausted all the local rogues as suspects. They're even getting unsolicited advice from members of the public, too. Apparently, two of our constables and the desk sergeant have been teased about our lack of results and given plenty of suggestions for the likely culprit. All of those are known to us and none fit the evidence. Plus, their own relatives, friends and even landladies have been quizzing them with as much tenacity as reporters.'

Brookland sighed. 'Tell them if they do come up with a viable subject, I'll be pleased to hear about them. They shouldn't need coaxing. And they should meet all forms of questioning with the same answer. "No comment." What else?'

'That MacDonald was practising escape routes to take subsequent to a robbery.'

Brookland whistled. 'I hadn't thought of that. Well, somebody has imagination, I'll say that for them. Add it to the list of possibilities. Check if the locations where the motorcycle was seen add up to a route past banks, post offices or jewellers, or even pawnbrokers. If it does, you'd better talk to our colleagues in Sussex. In fact, talk to them anyway, since they did us a good turn with the motorcycle sightings.'

'Right,' said Collins. 'That'll keep the lads occupied for a few hours...'

CHAPTER FIVE

"Police connect stolen motorcycle to murder of elderly lady

by *Wringford Gazette and Echo* reporter

Police are following up several promising leads in the murder of Dora Jenkins, the former Royal Ballet dancer, found dead in her home in Lower Broadwood on Saturday. They now believe a stolen Ariel motorcycle, last seen on Monday in Sussex, may have been used by a suspect in the case. A vase believed stolen from the deceased has yet to be found, and the police are making enquiries among pawnbrokers and others in an effort to discover if this item has been offered for sale."

- Wringford Gazette and Echo

Thursday morning was wet and overcast, but it didn't dampen Brookland's mood at all. He had gone home the previous evening with the knowledge that they were a step closer to their suspect's movements, even if they didn't know his motives. He and Collins were in agreement about

MacDonald; they may not yet know what he was up to, but his connection to Miller had brought him to their attention. He had borrowed and retained Miller's motorcycle, lied about informing Miller's parents, and suddenly vanished from sight. That in itself was worthy of attention; all three actions together had to mean something was going on, presumably nothing legal. Something would happen which would explain MacDonald's behaviour right enough; it was just a matter of time. Now, as Brookland sat in his office, drinking his tea and munching on a biscuit, he had the unshakeable feeling that something would happen today that would confirm they were after the right person at last.

Collins also went home in mildly better spirits, and for much the same line of reasoning, but on waking this morning he once more began to have serious doubts about MacDonald being the thief. He hadn't known Dora Jenkins, so how would he know about the vase? He didn't know Peter Miller's father worked for her, so borrowing the motorcycle must have been a coincidence. Which likely meant that whatever MacDonald was doing, it may have nothing to do with the case. Which is why he was consuming his cup of tea in the incident room, poring yet again over all the notes and looking for something he was sure he'd missed. Again.

Both Dale and Stevens had noticed the disparity in mood between their two superiors and were determined to find some way to help. Which is why the two men were sitting quietly in discussion in the small station kitchen. They had Dale's notebook between them, remaking lists of facts about MacDonald and the circumstances around the murder. Each was trying to think of questions they hadn't asked and noting things they might check on when another constable entered the room and handed Dale a sheet of paper. He shot to his feet and followed the latter out of the kitchen and in the direction of the front desk. Over his shoulder he said, 'Barry, tell the Sarge. Some lad saw Bracewell's car in an abandoned yard all weekend.'

❖

Some five minutes later, one Chief Inspector, one Detective Sergeant, a young lad and his father were seated in Brookland's office.

'So, David,' said Brookland, 'I'm Detective Chief Inspector Brookland, and this is Detective Sergeant Collins. I understand you're a car enthusiast? And you've seen a 1937 dark green Austin Seven parked in an unusual place? And you wrote down the licence plate?'

'Yes, sir.' David handed over a piece of paper neatly printed with a car registration number. 'It was parked all weekend in the yard of the old warehouse on West Street.' The boy was dressed in a local school uniform, and Brookland estimated him to be around twelve years of age. His father was around forty, thickset and dressed in casual clothes.

'And what made you think there was something odd about it?' Collins asked. 'It might belong to the owner of the warehouse.'

'My uncle just bought the warehouse, and it isn't his car, because that's a Morris Oxford. I told Dad, but when he looked on Monday evening, the car had gone. We asked Uncle Bill, he said it shouldn't have been there.'

Jeff Grey then spoke up. 'I worked nights this week, and David has been badgering me to bring him to report it to you. Fact is, I didn't expect anyone to be interested, but David thought it important, and it was at my brother's place, so here we are.'

'Thank you, Mr Grey. You were quite correct to come to us; we know who owns the car and we're glad to know where it was all weekend.'

'Was it stolen, Chief Inspector?' the boy asked excitedly. 'Or used in a bank robbery?'

Brookland smiled at the boy's enthusiasm. 'Not that we know. Why do you ask?'

'Well,' said the boy, 'it can't have been much use. One tyre was flat. It couldn't have travelled very far like that. But it must have been fixed again if it was gone Monday night.'

Brookland looked thoughtful. Then he stood

and reached into his pocket to draw out a shiny half-crown. 'David, your information has been very useful to us,' he said. 'And you've given me some new ideas too. Please accept my thanks and this half-crown for your excellent police work.' He handed it to the boy, whose eyes grew big as he stood to take it. 'Thank you,' he beamed, and looked at his father, who smiled at him, then looked up at Brookland and stood, reaching to shake the DCI's proffered hand.

'Thank you, too, Mr Grey, for bringing David to see us. He has been a great help to us today.'

'Well, I'm glad to hear that, Chief Inspector.'

'Sergeant Collins, please show Mr Grey and his son out.'

❖

After their witness left with his father to return to school, Brookland called Collins and Dale into his office.

'Well, that was interesting,' said Collins as they all trooped in. Brookland sat down on the corner of his desk and the others occupied the chairs in front.

'The problem we now have,' said Brookland,' is that we don't know what it means. Bracewell may just have left his car somewhere he thought safe because of the punctured tyre. He could have caught a train to... where was he?'

'Hawford, sir,' said Dale.

'Does a train go to Hawford?' asked Collins, looking at Dale, who immediately regained his feet and headed out of the office to fetch the station's copy of Bradshaw's guide. He returned a moment later, several leaflets tucked under his arm, the guide open in his hands and his finger on a page. Then he looked up.

'No.'

'Bus?'

Dale shuffled papers, compared timetables for a further minute. 'Yes. Eventually.'

'He could have been given a lift.' Brookland suggested. Collins looked at Dale, who looked confused.

'Don't worry, Dale, you can't check everything that way.' Brookland laughed.

Dale brightened. 'Should I ask Bracewell himself?'

'Not yet.' Brookland said. 'We don't want to ask the wrong question and risk giving away our endeavours. But it could be a point of interest. Or it could be a coincidence.'

'Coincidence, sir? Dale asked.

'He may not have intended to use his car to travel at all. If he was already expecting to travel with a colleague or companion, the car may have been left where a third party could find it and take it for repair.'

'Except that they didn't. At least, not until

after Monday evening, when he was back.' Collins pointed out. 'He made no mention of a work colleague, nor did the landlady of the B&B in Hawford.'

'Perhaps he got a lift from a motorist travelling in that direction, either part-way or through that town.' Dale suggested.

'Possibly,' said Brookland. 'But he would still need to get to the show somehow unless he knew he could walk there and back.'

'Other than a colleague on the paper, who would he know?' Collins asked. 'A journalist from another paper? A neighbour? A fellow boarder?'

Brookland shrugged. 'But he didn't leave the car at home, so he knew about the puncture. If he wanted somebody to repair it, he would have...' Brookland tailed off in thought. Then an idea struck him. 'Where's the nearest garage?'

❖

As it turned out, there were four garages within sensible walking distance; one did not carry out repairs, one had closed a month before with the death of the owner, and the remaining two were visited by constables at Collins' request.

By 5 pm, they had the explanation they were seeking. A mechanic with E. Green and Sons, a motor repair garage two streets away from the location of the abandoned vehicle and the furthest from the warehouse, remembered replacing a tyre for a gentleman who asked for his help on Monday afternoon. The repairman, a middle-aged, wiry fellow with horn-rimmed glasses was eager to help, and fetching his bicycle, the group headed back to the station. Collins and Brookland showed their witness to an interview room, while Dale took notes.

'I was just finishing the paperwork for the car I was working on,' said the mechanic, one Sam Harding by name. 'A young gentleman came in through the door and asked if I could replace a punctured tyre. The gentleman had tried to swap the tyre at the time, but it was dark and he couldn't fix it properly. He'd returned in daylight and taken a chance driving it the short distance to our garage. I inspected the replaced wheel, corrected it, and replaced the tyre on the spare. It took less than half an hour. He paid me, thanked me, and drove off.'

Collins had been thinking while Harding gave his statement. 'Did he give his reasons for leaving the car where he did?'

Harding scratched his head. 'Now that you come to mention it, he did. He said he wanted his girl to think he was away, so he could check up on her. He thought she was seeing someone else, and him being out of town, well, he thought she might go see this other feller. Anyway, he said he was wrong, she stayed at home all evening, and then when he tried to drive the car, he found he'd got a puncture. Sort of providential, really.'

How so?' asked Brookland?

'Well, if he hadn't been spying on his girl, he wouldn't have parked where he did and got that puncture. Providential, I call it.' Harding seemed to think that was amusing. 'Providential, that's what it was.'

'Yes, indeed. And you say this was - when?' Brookland enquired.

'Monday afternoon. He couldn't come earlier, he said, on account of he was at work.'

'Yes, of course. That makes sense,' said Brookland, standing. 'Well, thank you for coming in, Mr Harding. You've been very helpful.'

'One thing more, Mr Harding,' said Collins, producing a photograph from the shelf behind him. 'Is this the gentleman?' He showed the mechanic the borrowed photograph of Bracewell.

'Yes, that's Mr Peters.'

'Thank you, Mr Harding. The constable will show you out.' Dale, who was outside in the corridor, took his cue and directed Harding towards the station's reception area.

When he had left, Brookland said, 'Now, what do you make of that, Bob?'

Collins shrugged. 'He's definitely covering his tracks for some reason. I don't buy the excuse; that was for Harding's benefit, but the car was hidden for a reason. It wasn't just left there Sunday, but Saturday too. I wonder...' Collins headed out of the interview room and into the incident room. Brookland, puzzled, followed him.

'Yes, here it is.' Collins picked up the sheet he was looking for, handing it to Brookland. 'Nurse Gillespie said Bracewell took her home Friday night, so the car was fine then. He must have left it in the yard late Friday or early Saturday.'

Brookland frowned. 'No. It wasn't fine.'

Collins stared at him. Then his eyes widened. 'Melrose.'

Brookland nodded. 'Melrose said his burglar threw away his pick-locks in front of a car. An Austin Seven, he thought, with its lights on.'

'Bracewell parked it and got cigarettes out of a machine, but he didn't see PC Melrose or the thief, or see the pick-locks in front of his tyre!' Collins clamped a hand over his mouth. 'What bad luck. He knew he couldn't repair it in the dark, so he hid it, safely he hoped, until Monday. Too embarrassed to mention it, I suppose, or perhaps he thought it just wasn't relevant. He got it repaired, so it turned out all right.'

'True. He wouldn't have had time to get it fixed on Saturday. It doesn't appear anyone else noticed it. I don't suppose there's an outstanding summons... Dale?'

The constable stopped in the doorway on his way past and raised an eyebrow. 'Sir?'

'Bracewell's car - are there any warrants out on

it?'

'No, sir, nothing at all.'

Brookland nodded. ' Thank you. Add Mr Harding's statement to the timeline, Dale. We'll pick this up in the morning.'

CHAPTER SIX

"Police search residences in Dora Jenkins case
by *Wringford Gazette and Echo* reporter

It is now one week since the murder of former dancer Dora Jenkins, aged 82, of Lower Broadwood, but police have yet to make an arrest. They have searched the known residences for information as to the whereabouts of a suspect or suspects, as yet unnamed. It is not known if the enquiry has produced any items from the robbery."

- *Wringford Gazette and Echo*

Friday saw the Chief Inspector meeting with his bosses once again. He had been as truthful as he could be about their progress on the case, but even to himself it sounded rather thin. It was all still up in the air and he knew it. His superiors had expected the case to be closed by now, with a clear suspect in custody. Brookland was privately inclined to agree, but had stressed the unusual features of the case, the garden offering concealed from the road, and the placement of the windows away from neighbouring houses. He had even brought a sketch map and the list of possible clues. The DCS had gone through them and reluctantly conceded his point of view after Brookland had offered to turn the case over to his superior to resolve. The man had declined, just as Brookland knew he would. Detective Chief Superintendent Elden Marshall was a bureaucrat at heart and never much of a field detective. He had a better head for rules and procedure than for the intuition of the detective; he had long since accepted his role in life as that of manager rather than that of detective. Still, he had Brookland's respect as he was a good facilitator and always held his detectives in high esteem. He knew Marshall would present his information in a positive light to the Chief and could be relied upon to back his men. As Brookland had served with Scotland Yard when a DI, there was no question of bringing in an outsider to take charge, but Brookland had left with his own confidence rattled over the failure to progress the case further.

His return to the station around lunchtime was noted by WPC Harris, who swiftly brought a soothing cup of tea to her boss, to be rewarded in turn with a grateful smile and thanks from Brookland. He was standing in the incident room, staring at a map of the adjacent county. Dale had set coloured pins in the locations where Miller's motorcycle was seen, and those where Bracewell's motor car was seen. Brookland noted that they did not overlap, nor had he expected them to do so, but he was frustrated with the strange nature of the case; two vague suspects, both with partially corroborated alibis, just as one might expect from two young, single men, freely moving around the county. Staring at the pins didn't offer any insight. As for Bracewell's puncture, perhaps he had arranged a lift with a colleague after all and leaving the car where he did might simply have been a last-minute safety precaution rather than a guilty act. Perhaps he hadn't mentioned it simply because he didn't see it as relevant, or perhaps he had expected it to be repaired in his absence and didn't want to sound churlish to find it still unrepaired on his return. There was nothing factual to link either man directly to the murder.

Perhaps they were looking at it all wrong; MacDonald may well have intended to hand back the motorcycle on returning from work just as he had said he would, and then something had changed for him. Unless they found him, they might never know the truth. Bracewell's actions might have been connected to MacDonald; two acquaintances working together to - what? Steal, murder, leave for work and come back home? Brookland shook his head to clear it. He went in search of Collins, only to be told that he was out and found Constable Stevens looking for him in turn.

The visit to the auction house had produced only one further sketch, and that little better than the others; much to Stevens' frustration, one of MacDonald's former colleagues had shown more interest in the lady sketch artist than the subject they were trying to describe.

Stevens told Brookland that Collins had decided to review the evidence too, except he had returned to the crime scene with Dale as a second set of eyes. They intended to walk the crime scene and go through the sequence of events once more. Brookland silently wished them luck.

❖

Collins locked the door of the house belonging to the late Dora Jenkins. John Miller had loaned him the keys as Edward Jenkins had now appointed him caretaker. Collins had been amused at that; no doubt Jenkins intended to avoid journeying to and from his late aunt's home every time the police needed to verify something. Well, that suited him just fine: he found Jenkins' presence disquieting. The frequent police presence at his late aunt's home had been trying the solicitor's patience, and he was not shy about letting them know. Collins hadn't expected to find anything new at the crime scene, but he had hoped the visit might spark a few thoughts. As it happened, something did turn up in the person of Peter Miller.

Collins and Dale, having spent the better part of the morning searching the house for clues they might have missed before, turned their attention to the grounds of the house. A shout from the road made the two men straighten up in time to see Peter Miller striding up the driveway.

'Mr Miller, is something wrong?' Collins asked as the man arrived, out of breath, in front of him, obviously in a state of excitement.

'I've seen Hamish MacDonald!'

Collins and Dale exchanged glances. 'Where?'

'Last night, outside the pub. He was arguing with another man I didn't recognise when I drove down the street. I tried to follow him, but he was on foot and walked down a footpath between nearby houses. I drove around to the other end, but he was gone. I can show you if you like. I couldn't tell you earlier, because I was at work. I came home for lunch and saw your car so I came straight over.'

'We're finished here,' Collins said, handing the key to the house to Miller, who took it with a nod, 'so we could go now. When do you need to be back at work?'

'Half an hour,' Miller said. 'My motorcycle's on the drive behind your car.'

Miller started up his motorcycle and eased it around slowly into the road, giving Dale time to reverse out of the driveway after him. They followed the young man a short way up the road, watching and following his hand signals and turns until they arrived at a large public house set back from the road. Dale drove into a space nearby while Miller parked close to the building and dismounted, joining the two policemen as they walked towards him.

'He was standing here,' he indicated the spot in front of them, 'arguing with the man. I recognised his coat and hat. As I said, I tried to follow him, but by the time I had turned the motorcycle around, he was walking down that lane—,' Miller gestured to a footpath between two streets of terraced houses, '—and I lost him.'

'Well, never mind. Now we can narrow our search a bit. If he's on foot, he may have walked here, so we might get lucky with another sighting. Mr Miller, do you think you could give a description of the other man to our police artist?'

'Of course, Sergeant. I'll come down after I leave work at six, if that's all right?'

'Yes, thank you. I'll have him there when you arrive. And thank you for being so observant. You've been very helpful.'

Miller grinned and headed back to his motorcycle, while both policemen returned to their car. 'If we can get a good likeness of the other man, we might try showing the sketches to the landlord.' said Collins.

'Or come back for a pint this evening?' asked Dale.

Collins grinned. 'What you do on your own time is your business, Constable; just don't use police property, eh?'

It was Dale's turn to grin as he eased the car out into the road and back to the station.

❖

Brookland was waiting for his officers to return with some impatience. He had no new clues, statements or even gossip to occupy his thoughts, which were still dwelling on the earlier meeting with his superiors. He didn't want his chaffing to affect his men, and he certainly didn't want them distracted, so he forced himself to remain at his desk until Collins came to report the results of his excursion. Collins duly arrived at Brookland's door and cheerfully greeted his Chief Inspector.

'Hello, sir. Can you spare a minute?' The irony of this question wasn't lost on Brookland; he frowned suspiciously at his sergeant, uncomfortably aware that there was nothing much on his desk except a teacup in its saucer and an empty biscuit plate partly covering today's newspaper. His unoccupied mind and attention were more obvious than he would have wished.

'Dozens, as you so clearly noticed.' Brookland said snippily. 'I hope you've got something to improve this day for me.'

'As a matter of fact, I do.'

Brookland raised a questioning brow as Collins slid into the seat across from him and launched into a long tale describing the fruitless additional search of the murdered woman's home.

'Then, just as we walked away from the house to return the key to Miller Senior, his son quickly approached us with some interesting news.' Brookland, who had forced himself to listen attentively and without comment, left elbow on the desk to support his face, now added his other elbow and stared at his junior officer with his face in both hands.

'And?' Brookland urged. Collins noted his senior officer's mood and wisely continued without further delay.

'Peter Miller saw MacDonald outside the White Oak public house, talking loudly with another older man. He showed us the location, and Dale is organising a sketch artist to assist Miller to create a portrait of the other man, tonight. We thought we might show the sketches to the landlord, perhaps the customers too. I also gave Dale permission to visit said pub after shift to see if either man returns tonight.'

'You think they might?'

'I thought Dale's idea had merit, but I'm not optimistic. We've no reason to assume either went inside, but it's worth a try. Oh, and one more thing - MacDonald was on foot.'

'You think he lives nearby?'

'He cut down a nearby lane which suggests local knowledge and proximity to the pub.'

'And the other man?'

'Miller lost him when he drove away in the opposite direction. It was too distant for him to see anything more.'

'Tell Dale he can have his covert operation tonight - let him off shift an hour early and tell him just to observe. Impress on him that he is not to pursue either man without assistance. If he does spot one or the other, he's to telephone the station and call out a car to help. I don't want him going unarmed into trouble.'

'Understood, sir.' Collins stood and left Brookland's office. Brookland followed, walking into the incident room to make notes. Collins would write up the events presently, but Brookland wanted a few notes now. He looked at the location of the pub on the wall map, and added a pin to represent the sighting. After a second's pause, he added another pin for the second man.

At 6:20 pm precisely, Peter Miller walked through the doors of the Wringford Police Station just as Sergeant Collins walked out of the incident room and headed towards the front of the station to await his arrival.

'Mr Miller.' Collins smiled at the visitor and extended his hand to shake that of the younger man. 'Thank you for coming.'

'Of course, Sergeant. I just hope I can be of some help.'

'I'm sure you can. This way, please. We're ready for you.' Collins indicated the way to one of the interview rooms where a police artist was waiting. Miss Peters being unavailable, a colleague had offered to turn up.

'Mr Miller, this is Mr Warboys,'

'Hello,' Miller said and held out his hand to shake that of the man who had now risen from his seat at the table to return the gesture. A short, balding man in his late fifties, he wore a corduroy jacket and dark trousers. Miller settled into the seat Warboys indicated across from him.

'Mr Warboys has agreed to try to capture both men's portraits, not just our unknown   second party. Would you try again to describe Hamish MacDonald's appearance? There may be something else you can add this time.' said Collins. 'When you're satisfied, please do the same for the other man. Also, a description of both sets of clothes, if you can?'

'I'll do my best, Sergeant,' replied Miller amiably, twisting in his seat to reply to Collins, before once more returning to face the artist opposite.

'Now,' said Warboys in a clear voice. 'Let's begin.'

Collins closed the door and walked back to the incident room. Brookland had gone home at six o'clock; Collins would leave when they had Miller's sketches ready. He walked toward the front of the station once more and sought Constable Stevens, who was making tea for himself. A brief conversation followed, and Collins returned to his desk to await Cyril Warboys' skilled efforts.

Half an hour later, Collins had his sketches and was saying goodbye to both Miller and Warboys. Mindful of the fact that Dale had not seen the portraits, and therefore did not know what either of their suspects looked like, he had arranged with Constable Stevens to take the sketches to a local printer's shop in order to have them copied before taking a set to Constable Dale at home. He hoped Dale would be careful in his enquiries; a part of him hoped neither man would show and the landlord or a customer might provide the information they sought. Another part hoped the unknown man would appear and Dale might discover something of value. He finally headed home, having resolved to let his constable do his job, then found himself making a U-turn only to speed off in the opposite direction.

❖

Collins parked his car a few minutes' walk from the White Oak and ducked into a bus shelter to hide in the shadows. He felt uncomfortable skulking in the dark as if spying on his own man, but rationalised his feelings by telling himself he was simply providing backup for his officer. He waited in the gloom for a good twenty minutes before he saw Dale ride along on his motorcycle dressed in a leather overcoat, gloves, helmet and goggles. He watched Dale stop and dismount, jerk the motor-cycle onto its stand, then walk away, pulling off his gloves and raising his goggles as he entered the pub. He looked much transformed from the young man on the job that Collins was used to seeing, and he approved. Collins counted to fifty in his head, then left his hiding place and walked across to the pub, walking into the dark corner as a car drove past. Once it had gone, he moved nearer to a window which was left ajar owing to the balmy night.

He saw Dale order a pint and strike up a conversation with the barman, a man close to his own age. He watched Dale lean back on the bar and take a sweeping look around the room, then back to the barman and finally his drink. After a few more minutes, Dale straightened, picked up his pint and walked to another part of the pub. Collins could vaguely hear Dale's voice, but could no longer see him. The barman looked in a Dale's direction, then at a customer who had approached the bar. Collins decided to move to another window for a chance to see what Dale was now doing; the sudden noise of billiard balls smacking together suggested Dale was watching or even playing the game. Collins moved quietly and ducked under the window only to see headlights in front of him. He slid behind a bench and hoped the headlights wouldn't reveal his hiding place. The car stopped a little way off, the headlights and taillights were extinguished and the doors opened and shut. Moments later, the pub door opened and shut. Collins breathed a sigh and straightened himself at the side of the other window. He cursed to himself when he found he still couldn't see Dale, or hear him.

Suddenly, Collins saw Dale walk past the window, billiard cue in hand. Collins flattened himself against the outside wall and held his breath, but Dale had returned to the game. The sound of female laughter met Collins' ears, and he wondered if Dale had forgotten his assignment and decided to enjoy his time in the pub instead. He briefly considered entering the pub himself, only to dismiss the idea. He had trusted Dale to carry out his task; to reveal himself would gain nothing and probably embarrass the young constable. Collins decided to wait ten more minutes. Twenty-five minutes later, he heard Dale give a cheery 'Goodnight' and moments later the door opened once more.

'Good evening, Sarge. Fancy seeing you here!'

Collins winced as he heard Dale's quietly mocking greeting.

'All right, Mike, so you know I was watching you. No need for sarcasm. Did you learn anything useful?'

'As a matter of fact, yes. I learned the name of the man talking to MacDonald.'

CHAPTER SEVEN

"Local man sought in murder of elderly lady

by Wringford Gazette and Echo reporter

Police are still making enquiries in the Dora Jenkins case. Although they have not confirmed the identity of their suspects, it is believed that they are concentrating their efforts on one local man."

-Wringford Gazette and Echo

Saturday morning saw Brookland, Collins and Dale seated in the incident room with the sketch of the unknown man and a pile of folders on the table before them. Dale had been giving a summary of the previous evening's events; clearly, he was enjoying regaling them with his narrative.

'So, after a few minutes, the door at the back of the room opens, and in comes a young girl of around twelve years old. She racks the snooker balls and proceeds to break. I wander over to watch, thinking I can lounge around easier if I'm apparently watching something. The next moment, the young girl challenges me to a game! I agree and introduce myself; she does the same. Her name is Susan; she's the landlord's granddaughter. I ask her if she lives there; she says she's staying with her grandfather while her parents are abroad. They're buyers for a London store and have to travel a lot, she says. Anyhow, she knows most of the regulars - and beats them sometimes it seems. I took a chance on telling her that I'm a detective looking for a villain-' Brookland raises his eyebrow at that '-and can I trust her to keep it quiet?'

'And?' urges Collins, amused.

'And she says "Yes, who is he?" I tell her that's what I'm trying to find out, I only have a sketch and a description. She asks to see them and smiles. "I know him," she says, pointing to the sketch of the heavily-set unknown man and promptly pots another ball in the corner pocket. 'Well?' I ask. "It's Crusher. Crusher Evans. He works for Mr Jarman."'

Brookland whistled. 'If Jarman's sending his thug after MacDonald, there must be money involved. Did your young lady say if he's a regular?'

Dale's expression froze on his face. 'Mine, sir? I hardly think...'

'No, Constable, I don't either. What did your young acquaintance say?'

'That her grandfather knows 'Crusher' Evans and also Trevor Jarman, but that she hasn't met Jarman.'

'Jarman's a bookie. What's his connection to her

grandfather? Does he owe Jarman too?' asked Collins.

'I don't know, Sarge. She only saw Evans twice, and her grandfather served him both times. She seemed to think her grandfather was perfectly friendly; perhaps he doesn't know Jarman's real business?'

'Well,' said Collins, 'we'll need to find Evans and see if he can clear up this business with Mac-Donald. We still need to charge MacDonald with unlawfully retaining Miller's motor motorcycle. We're still no closer to connecting him to the old lady's murder until we can find a reason beyond his association with Miller, and if he knew of the old lady's collection and the layout of the house.'

'All right, Dale,' said Brookland. 'You did a good job last night; enjoy your weekend. Don't go near the pub for a day or two until we've had a chance to talk to Evans.'

'Thank you, sir. I'll see you Monday, then. 'Bye, Sarge.'

With that, he left the room and the station.

Brookland stood, and Collins got to his feet too. 'I'll get someone to contact Jarman and see if we can get a word with Evans. I'll let you know if we learn anything of interest, sir.'

'Thanks, Bob. I'd appreciate that. And now I have to battle the blackfly on my roses.' Brookland picked up his coat and walked from the room.

Collins followed him to the front of the station and collared a constable, instructing him to find out Jarman's address. A few minutes later, he too left the station, coat in hand, and accompanied by Constable Stevens.

❖

Finding 'Crusher' Evans wasn't as difficult a task as Collins had feared. The man himself was sitting in a chair in the small front lobby of the second-floor office suite above the local newsagent's shop. A large, bullet-headed man of around thirty-five, Evans was dressed in a dark suit. His shoes were scuffed at the toes; Collins wondered if it was from kicking somebody.

As the two men came through the doorway, Evans dropped the sports section of a newspaper onto the floor and came forward.

'Mr Jarman ain't in today.'

'That's okay, Evans. We came to see you,' said Collins. Evans eyed the uniformed Constable suspiciously.

'Wot for?'

Collins introduced himself and his colleague before pulling a folded paper out of his inside jacket pocket.

'We are looking for this man in connection with a theft. We have witnesses who saw you with him last night at the White Oak.'

'So?' said Evans, his face unreadable.

'So, what is his name, where does he live, and what was your business with him last night?'

Evans was about to offer a further monosyllabic response when the door of the office across from them opened and an older, grey-haired man in a smart blue suit walked into the lobby. He smiled pleasantly at the two visitors and held out a hand to Collins.

'Ah, Detective Sergeant Collins, Constable Stevens. Trevor Jarman. I hope Crusher here has been helpful?'

'As a matter of fact, no. He informed us you were out, and he hasn't answered our questions yet.'

Jarman tutted. 'Crusher, the Constabulary is seeking information, and it is our duty to assist them.'

Evans looked warily at his boss; Jarman encouraged him with a wave of his hand.

"'is name's 'amish MacDonald. I 'aven't found out exactly where 'e lives; 'e gave up his old flat, but it's somewhere in Jubilee Walk, back 'o the White Oak.' He looked at Jarman again, but his boss spoke.

'Mr MacDonald took out a loan through my financial services company, and he has only made one repayment. Mr Evans was reminding him of his responsibilities and requesting a further payment.'

Stevens scoffed. Collins met his eye and smiled.

Turning back to Jarman, he said, 'Just how much does he owe you, Mr Jarman?'

'Around £400, Detective Sergeant. And I can show you the contract if you like?'

'Perhaps in the future, Mr Jarman. Do you know Mr MacDonald's profession?'

'A printer, I believe.'

'And the reason for the loan?'

'I believe it was for a motor car, Detective Sergeant.'

Collins nodded. 'Thank you, Mr Jarman, Mr Evans, for your help in this matter. Goodbye.'

'Goodbye, Detective Sergeant.'

Once back at the station, Collins made himself a cup of tea and munched his lunchtime sandwiches. He wrote up his interview with Evans and Jarman, returned the other paperwork to the files and added the entry of Jubilee Walk as a possible address to MacDonald's sparse file notes. A check of the local street directory revealed that Jubilee Walk was one of the older roads and not one of the wealthiest. Fifty-six houses. How many were boarding houses? A few, probably. Somebody would have to check the district records. A job for one of the more methodical constables, no doubt. Collins walked out of the incident room and found Constable Stevens finishing his lunch.

'Barry, find out how many of the houses in Jubilee Walk have lodgers currently staying in them.'

'Right, Sarge.'

Collins was about to turn away when a thought struck him.

'Did we get confirmation of Bracewell's address?'

'Only the postman's statement that one J Bracewell was the recipient of letters there. The neighbours didn't know who the occupant was - the house is set back a piece and the nearest neighbours are new to the area.'

Collins frowned. 'Send somebody out to try again. Forget the house for the moment, I want to see that for myself. Talk to the neighbours again, perhaps the local shops to see if they've delivered newspapers or groceries, things like that. We really do need to find out why Bracewell left his car in the yard all weekend; I don't buy that story he gave the garage mechanic. It doesn't fit what we know of Nurse Gillespie at all.'

'Unless he has a second girlfriend?' Stevens suggested, hesitantly.

Collins opened his mouth and shut it again. 'Or maybe we should stop guessing and ask him this time. See what your colleagues can turn up.'

'Yes, Sarge.'

This time Collins returned to the incident room and his notes. He looked up at the clock on the wall. It was now almost two o'clock. Around fifty minutes later, Stevens walked into the room and handed Collins a sheet of paper.

'Only four houses have lodgers, and one of those is a large house subdivided into six flats. About twenty people in all, although he could just be staying with someone, not renting,' Stevens added.

Collins nodded. 'That's if Crusher is right. If he isn't, there are two more streets he could have walked to. It's not very helpful. I don't think going door-to-door is an option yet. We'll have to leave that as a last resort.'

Stevens nodded and left, returning to his desk at the front of the station.

Collins added the sheet to the existing papers, wrote a few further notes, and decided after fifteen minutes that no more could be squeezed from that day's efforts. He stretched, got to his feet and picked up his coat, folding it over his arm, and headed out of the door.

He found Stevens and informed him he was leaving for the day.

'Very good, Sarge. Will you be in tomorrow?'

'No, Barry. The station is all yours until Monday unless something turns up. Goodbye.'

'Goodbye, Sarge. Have a good weekend.'

'I will, Barry. Have a good watch.'

Collins headed away from the station, but not

in the direction of his home. He headed out to Bracewell's address, aware that he would soon encounter whoever Stevens sent to canvas the neighbours once more. He parked a short way down the road, then walked the rest of the way. Satisfying himself that he was not observed, he rang the doorbell; once, twice, three times. After receiving no reply in that time, he unlatched the side gate and investigated the rear of the property. A small garage lay at the end of the driveway; having found himself alongside its windowed length, Collins peered in. There was a black Wolseley 4/50 parked inside: not Bracewell's car, obviously. He moved away, towards the windows at the rear of the house. Peering into the first, he saw a kitchen, neat and tidy. The second window revealed a lounge, equally neat and tidy. Collins tried to picture Bracewell as the occupant; no, that was unlikely. This must belong to an older brother, uncle or even parents. Collins took a final look around, searched in vain for a hidden spare key, and reluctantly decided that if someone was staying here or minding the place in its owners' absence, it wasn't James Bracewell.

As he walked back to his vehicle, he was bemused to see another black Wolseley draw up. This one was more familiar: a police vehicle from the station. He waited until the driver had parked and stepped out. Then he smiled as he saw the driver: WPC Louise Harris.

Making his presence known by walking alongside, he called out cheerfully, 'Good afternoon, Constable.'

Louise' face broke into a smile at the sight of him. 'Are you checking on me, Detective Sergeant Collins?' She spoke teasingly, but Collins didn't want her to be concerned.

'Absolutely not, Constable. I simply wanted to see the house for myself. And I have. It's not occupied by our subject, of that I'm sure, but may belong to a relative.' He conveyed to her what he'd seen and the inferences he'd drawn. She nodded in agreement, and Collins knew she would go and see for herself once he'd left.

'Our chap is sounding more suspicious by the day,' she said, 'and I thought I'd see what a woman's touch might get out of the neighbours. A little gossip here and there, perhaps, and a trip to the local shops afterwards. I could find out which milkman they use, too.'

'That's a good idea, Louise. I never thought of that!' Collins laughed approvingly. 'Well, you obviously have the matter in hand, so I'll leave you to it. Good hunting!'

'Goodbye, Sergeant, and thank you!' She smiled warmly and walked to the gate of the nearest house, passing through and closing it behind her. Collins walked back to his own vehicle, and this time drove home. A short report to add to his files for Monday and the rest of the weekend was his.

CHAPTER EIGHT

Monday morning brought its share of ringing telephones and foot traffic, but none of it relevant to the murder case. Two drunk-and-disorderlies, a stolen bicycle (later recovered from a front garden three streets away) and a missing person report took up most of the morning for the constables. Brookland barely had time to read through Collins' and Harris' reports from Friday as Collins fielded questions from citizens at the front desk while the constables were occupied elsewhere. Brookland too answered a few enquiries from newspapers and finally, the phones stopped their ringing around midday.

'Lunchtime,' said Brookland. 'Even criminals stop for lunch, apparently.'

'Collins laughed. 'Careful, sir, you'll jinx it.'

'Well, you can have the next reporter, Bob. Funny they're suddenly interested in the Dora Jenkins case. Must be a slow news day. Up until now...' he tailed off and went quiet.

'Sir?'

Brookland looked around for Monday's *Gazette*.

He grabbed it and turned the pages, scanning quickly. Then he looked for the previous edition and scanned that. Then he picked up several copies of the Echo and scanned those. Collins watched him with a frown on his face. Finally, he could no longer stay quiet.

'What is it, sir?

'It's not there today. Why isn't it there today?'

'What, sir?'

Brookland looked up at Collins. 'Every day there's been a short piece on the murder. Only a few paragraphs. Now, today, nothing.' He handed the previous papers over to Collins, folding them to show the article. Collins read them, then looked around for the previous newspapers that Brookland had perused. After a quarter of an hour's effort, they had all the articles clipped and taped onto a sheet.

'So here we are, one piece per day in the *Gazette*, one in the *Echo* then nothing today, and two reporters from the *Echo* and the *Gazette* phone us.' Brookland paused and looked at his notes. He looked for the newspapers' contact number and reached for the phone, asking the switchboard operator for first one then the second reporter.

Finally, he put the phone down.

Brookland looked up at Collins and said, 'According to our two reporters, the reason they called in for news was that their editor told them.

They'd both been given the assignment when the previous reporter didn't show up for work and couldn't be found. Their editor wanted to see which one could get a scoop, although he hadn't expected both would ring up within the hour.'

'Who was the original reporter?' Collins asked, a sinking feeling in the pit of his stomach that he already knew the answer.

'James Bracewell.'

❖

Collins stared at Brookland as he made this statement. 'Bracewell has been writing pieces about the murder of someone he actually knew?'

'That's how it appears. And now he's missing.'

'Since when?' asked Collins.

'He was at work on Friday, was off all weekend, and was expected in this morning. However, Eve Gillespie rang the editor at 9 am to ask if he was there; she hadn't seen him since Friday evening and was due to meet him for lunch on Sunday. He failed to show, and when she hadn't heard from him by this morning, decided to call him at work. The editor says he hasn't appeared and was wondering if he should call us when I called him. I think we should consider the possibility that he has disappeared.'

Collins went in search of Dale and met the man walking towards Brookland's office. Collins stepped back to allow him to enter.

'Ah, good. Constable Dale, please put out a flash for James Bracewell, who may be missing. He hasn't been seen since Friday and hasn't turned up to work today. He missed a lunch date with Miss Gillespie and hasn't contacted her. You have the registration of his car?'

'Yes, sir. I gather from Policewoman Harris that he's not at the address he gave us.'

'No, Constable, and never has been.'

'Shall I concentrate the search around Lower Broadwood?'

'Why there?' asked Brookland.

'Because WPC Harris believes he's relocated there. It's in her report, sir.'

Brookland sighed. 'I haven't finished reading her report yet, so I'm a little behindhand...' He gestured for Dale to continue.

'Well, according to Constable Harris, she spoke to the neighbours and local shopkeepers about the house in Ivy Lane. They informed her that the Bracewells were an older couple, frequently away. The newspapers were on hold, and they knew of no lodgers or relatives living there. The dairy confirmed the milk was on hold for a month. A friend in another street has a key and checks on the house from time to time.'

Collins interrupted, 'Fine, but why do you both think he's moved to Lower Broadwood now?'

'Because his car was spotted near the station on

Sunday by one of the Transport constables making enquiries about a gang of thieves stealing from passengers on trains. He remembered the licence number, but the driver drove away before he could identify him. He drove off in the direction of the pub, not towards Wringford.'

'Which pub?' asked Brookland.

'The White Oak.'

'The pub where Crusher met MacDonald?' queried Collins. 'That's an odd coincidence.'

'Yes. But the constable didn't see him turn in so he could have driven past.' Dale warned.

'Or driven down another road nearby.' Collins wondered aloud. He walked out of Brookland's office and into the incident room. A few moments later, he returned with a map of the area and spread it across Brookland's already littered desk. Brookland moved to stand at his shoulder, and Dale moved around to his other side. The map showed several residential areas within reach of the pub both by car and foot, but most were across the main road, not close to the pub.

'We did wonder if the two men were working together.' Collins reminded them.

'But we couldn't find anything that might link them together,' Dale said. 'Not a job, not a residence, nothing.'

'Nor have we found any witnesses who saw them together,' added Brookland.

'In fact,' said Collins thoughtfully, 'nobody who knows Bracewell seems to know MacDonald.'

'Bob?'

Collins stepped back and headed out of the door once again. He returned with the sketches of MacDonald and the photo of Bracewell. Placing them side by side over the map, he compared them. Brookland and Dale stared at the two likenesses.

'Good grief!' Dale burst out. 'It could be the same man!'

'There's a similarity, I'll admit,' said Brookland, considerably calmer than he felt at that point, 'but unless we can catch him, we can't identify him from these. We need our witnesses to do that for us.' Brookland picked up the two sheets and walked to the front of the station. His officers all stopped their actions and turned to see what he wanted.

'All of you take a look at these pictures. It appears two of our suspects may indeed be one man with two identities. We are going to have to review all we know about them in the light of this new information, but I don't want this to be known outside this station. Continue to search for James Bracewell under that name. Constable Dale is to be kept informed of developments - report to him anything you learn.' Nods and murmurs of assent answered this command. 'Dale, go ahead and take a team to canvas for Bracewell or MacDonald's lodgings in Jubilee Walk. If you find the place, call in for the lab team. See what you can find there, get photographs, take prints and speak to the landlord, the neighbours, everyone.'

'Sir.'

Brookland headed back to his room to read WPC Harris' report more carefully.

A short while later, having thoroughly read and digested WPC Harris' equally thorough report, Brookland took it into the incident room. There he found Collins making fresh notes on a sheet of blank paper. Collins had the files on Bracewell and MacDonald spread out to one side and was making a timeline of their movements in black and red ink. Brookland waited until Collins was aware of his presence before speaking; he did not want to interrupt Collins' flow of thought.

Collins ignored his superior until he had every point plotted, then he straightened up and turned to Brookland.

'Does it make sense, Bob?' asked Brookland, once he had his colleague's attention.

'Yes. They were only ever seen by different people at times that fit. The business with the motorcycle makes sense now. However, we still don't know why he chased all over the county that weekend.'

'What about alibis? Bracewell as MacDonald was seen at home by Miller in his previous flat that evening and only left the next morning.'

'I know. But the rest fits the timeline.' Collins tapped the sheet with his finger.

'Let's go over the whole thing in order then. Perhaps we'll see something we missed this time,' said Brookland.

Collins picked up his pens and started a fresh sheet. 'All right. Bracewell and Nurse Gillespie are in the pub on Friday night. Miss Jenkins is still alive. Bracewell spots the man at the bar, hurries Nurse Gillespie home. That's just before 10 pm.'

'Right,' said Brookland. 'She said nothing about a problem with the car; that must have happened after he dropped her at home. He must have formulated a plan of sorts, then realised the tyre had a puncture. Whether he intended to seek out Miller since he obviously knew where he lived or simply came across him by accident, we don't know. Either way, it was fortuitous; he stashed the car in the abandoned yard, out of sight, the motorcycle somewhere near his flat.'

'Exactly,' Collins agreed. 'Miller takes him to his flat. He evidently comes out again, unseen, several hours later. He enters Dora Jenkins' house, murders her and steals the vase. He returns home, still unseen, only to leave again, visibly, at around 10 am the next morning. The motorcycle must be close by, but not obvious.'

'And he spends the weekend carrying out his assignment and chasing around the countryside,' said Brookland.

'Only to return on Monday, get his car fixed and carry on as if nothing had happened,' added Collins.

'But something did happen, Bob, to propel him into action.' Brookland pointed out.

'Did it? Or was it already planned? He did have two identities,' said Collins.

'Yes, but you're forgetting the incident in the pub,' reminded Brookland.'He was under stress; he needed money to repay Jarman. He saw somebody in the pub and got out of there as fast as he could - probably Crusher or another of Jarman's thugs - and that's what started this ball rolling.'

'He must have thought his life was in danger,' Collins said sympathetically. 'The theft seemed a fast way to extricate himself. Until it became more complicated.'

'She surprised him, Bob. He didn't expect that, I'm sure. But now we have to find him.'

❖

Brookland spent the next fifteen minutes on the telephone to his superiors, informing them that they now knew who their main suspect was, but could not find their man, or prove his guilt.

In the meantime, Collins had caught up with his constables' enquiries, and learned that Bracewell was nowhere to be found; his car was also missing, suggesting he had either hidden it yet again or was in it; a check of his place of work, the pubs he frequented, Eve Gillespie's home and even Dora Jenkins' house revealed no clue as to Bracewell's location. Collins would wait for Dale to return from finding Bracewell's new home, but he guessed they would not find anything useful. He personally rang other police stations within a fifty-mile radius to ask them to watch for their suspect, adding Bracewell's car's registration number to the description.

That done, he returned to the incident room to think. He tried to put himself in their suspect's shoes. A fresh round of threats - the need for money - the stolen vase to be fenced - their man had abandoned his job, at least for the present, but was he running or simply trying to save himself from harm? If he was running, he could be heading for a port to take passage on a ship, a private airfield, or a train to the Continent. If trying to raise funds, he could be anywhere but would return at some point if he managed to raise the money to pay off Jarman.

Collins sat bolt upright, an idea occurring to him. When Brookland emerged from his office to look for his deputy, he found Collins scribbling notes on a fresh sheet of paper.

'Where are we, Bob?' Do we have any news on Bracewell?' he asked hopefully.

Collins spun to face him. 'I'm still awaiting news they've found Bracewell's new lodgings, but I had an idea.'

'Go on.'

'We know Bracewell needs money to pay off Jarman. What we don't know is whether he has given up trying and fled, or has succeeded and intends to return. He doesn't yet know we suspect him of the murder.'

'With you so far,' said Brookland, not certain where this was going.

'All right. We can't find him, but can we make him come to us?'

Brookland looked blankly at his Detective Sergeant. 'Why would he come to us?'

'Because he no longer needed to run.' Collins began to grin. 'What if his debt was cancelled, and he thought he was in the clear?'

Brookland smiled. 'He'd reappear. But are you suggesting we pay off the debt? That's a lot of money.'

'My thought was that Edward Jenkins could be persuaded to donate the cash. Then I thought of something else,' Collins stated.

'He might find that acceptable,' agreed Brookland, 'What was your other idea? And how do we apprise Bracewell of the change in circumstances?'

'Well,' said Collins, indicating his notes, 'I've been trying out some ideas for newspaper advertisements. Bracewell is a journalist, so it's fair to say he reads newspapers too. He's bound to be familiar with the idea of a notice in the classified section. Supposing we place a notice to suggest Jarman has been arrested, along with his boys, and that we also have a suspect in custody for the Jenkins murder. That might be enough to get him to return.'

Brookland thought for a moment. 'It could work, but unless Jarman is willing to put his business on hold, he'll get wind of the lie and object. Plus, our own people read newspapers too. They'd spot it straight away.'

'Yes, I thought of that. Plus, we would need the advertisement to appear in most national papers too.' Collins sunk back into his chair, disappointment all too evident on his face.

'Never mind, Bob. It was a good thought, and maybe we could improve upon it, make it work. I'll put the kettle on.'

❖

Through the afternoon, Collins and Brookland monitored the constables' efforts to find Bracewell. Both had in their time carried out a good deal of door-to-door enquiries and knew only too well how long it might take, even assuming their information was correct. They knew they had little evidence to connect to him; a few smudged shoe-prints and the only witness dead. They had to define the exact chain of events and build a solid case for the prosecution; any doubts or gaps in the timing and their case could collapse. They did have gaps: Bracewell had left no firm evidence and only being arrested in possession of the vase would be sufficient. Brookland was beginning to feel the full weight of their task settling on his shoulders. Collins was equally low in spirit; he had gone over every piece of information they had and it was patchy at best. He got up and took their empty cups to the station kitchen to make more tea for both of them. Privately he felt like adding something stronger.

Around five o'clock, Dale appeared in the doorway.

'Sirs, we've located Bracewell's new lodgings in Jubilee Walk. It's No. 27.'

Collins and Brookland looked at each other and grinned in relief. 'I suppose it's too much to hope he was there?' said Brookland.

'No, sir, he wasn't. Hasn't been seen since yesterday morning. And there's not much left behind except a stack of newspapers and some rubbish. No clothes or personal items. He was paid up to Friday, according to the landlady, under the name Jack Burrows. He had a suitcase; that's gone too.'

'And we're none the wiser. What about his car, Constable? Was it parked nearby?'

'No, sir, nobody saw a car.'

'He could be on foot. Perhaps he intended to take a train - he was seen at the train station on

Sunday and he had his car then,' said Collins.

'Where has the car been and is he in it today? Has he purchased a ticket?' Brookland looked up at Dale.

'Dale, send someone to show his photograph at the station_'

'Already did that, sir, after he was spotted yesterday. We asked the staff to look out for him, but not to alarm him if they do see him.'

'Did you now! Well done, Dale! My compliments to your colleagues too.'

Dale grinned. 'I'll pass your words along, sir,' he said, clearly delighted.

'If the railway staff have been on the lookout for him, he probably hasn't left yet. I wonder why not? Lack of money or an appointment here somewhere?' Collins mused.

'Dale, get our men to keep a sharp eye out for that car when they're on their beats, and if they pass a car showroom or garage, they're to ask if one like it has been brought in. And tell them if they have any other ideas where to look, to follow those up as well.'

'Yes, sir.' Dale grinned again and disappeared to put the word out.

Brookland turned back to Collins.

'Bob, where else might he have gone? I think we can rule out London Airport unless he knows a local pilot, which I doubt. The river?'

'Well,' Collins started, 'there's his father...'

Brookland stared at him. 'You think Joey Mac-Donald is going to talk to us?'

'Probably not. But the probation service might know what Joey's been up to since his release.'

'Perhaps, but I doubt it.' Brookland reached for his teacup and drained it, replacing it in the saucer before continuing. 'But one of his former associates might. I'll phone Brighton police and have someone check on them for us.'

Collins had a sudden flash of inspiration and whooped 'France!'

'Why France?' Brookland asked, 'You think he'd head to Brighton then France? We don't know if he has a passport.'

Collins darted out of the door to find Dale, almost running into a constable approaching the open door. Brookland looked up expectantly.

'Sir, you have a telephone call.'

Brookland hung up the phone and leaned back in his chair. He was still in that position when Collins appeared in the doorway. He had looked for the DCI in the incident room where he had last seen him, but the room was empty. Wandering down the hallway, Collins looked for his superior in his own office and paused at the sight of Brookland deep in thought. He waited a moment or two, recognising Brookland's need for reflection. When

Brookland looked up and saw Collins, he straightened and stood up to face him.

'I just had a conversation with Brighton police,' he said. 'They did have a temporary address for Joey MacDonald, but apparently, he hasn't been seen there since the day after he got out of prison. Nothing left behind, either. So that washes out. I asked them about known associates; they already spoke to those they knew about who are still at large; apparently, nobody knows anything.'

'Which translates as: if they do, they're not talking,' finished Collins.

Brookland nodded. 'I've put in a call to the prison; the warden's office will see what they have on MacDonald. But the questions still remain: does Hamish know where to look for his father and is he looking for him?'

Collins brightened. 'We do have one new piece of information. I confirmed that, as Bracewell, he has a passport, and it's current.'

'His father too?'

'No, not currently.'

'Well, that opens up one possibility, certainly. Ring Brighton police again, just in case he heads for the continent. They can alert the ports, although he could still slip away on a private boat. And there's the possibility of heading to Ireland, or Southampton.' Brookland sighed, and looked at his watch. 'I'm going home, Bob. I'll see you tomorrow, but call me if we have any positive news.'

'I will. Good night, sir.'

CHAPTER NINE

Brookland walked into the station late on Tuesday morning to find himself in the midst of a blue maelstrom. He skirted around the uniforms and headed for the safety of his office only to find his Detective Sergeant using his telephone. Brookland left Collins to his own devices and walked into the incident room. There he found DC Dale copying locations onto a pair of county maps. Dale became aware of the senior officer's presence and straightened.

'What's going on, Dale? The station's in an uproar, and my Sergeant has made himself free of my telephone.'

'It's Bracewell. Or MacDonald, sir. We think we know what he's doing!'

A smile broke across Brookland's face. 'All right, Let's have it.' Dale opened his mouth to speak and closed it again as Collins entered the room. He must have heard the conversation because he nodded to Dale.

'Go on, Constable.'

'Right. Well, we got a call first thing this morning from a travel agency in town. The owner had a visit yesterday from one of our constables enquiring about Bracewell. One of his employees was out at the time, so he wasn't there when our man came in. The owner duly asked his clerk, who remembered a man purchasing a ticket for Wednesday evening's ferry crossing to Dieppe from Newhaven, via the Victoria to Brighton train. With all the customers he deals with, the clerk wasn't sure, but thought the man in the photograph could be the one who bought that ticket. The owner thought it worth the effort to call us this morning.'

'What makes you think it's Bracewell?' Brookland asked. 'It could be a coincidence.'

'They don't get asked for ferry tickets to Dieppe very often, and the ticket was one way.'

Brookland nodded. 'I admit, that sounds promising, but...'

'The man asked if he could purchase a railway ticket into London from there rather than the station, in case of queues,' interrupted Collins, 'and on being told no, the man was visibly worried. That's why the clerk remembered the conversation.'

'Fine. Do we have anyone at the station now?'

'No. If you remember, I sent someone out on Sunday to question the staff, and to telephone if they saw anyone resembling Bracewell/MacDonald. I haven't heard anything yet. Problem is, we don't know if he will use the train or a bus, or get a lift or...'

It was Brookland's turn to interrupt. 'He has a car. He'll use that to get to Brighton, surely?'

'No, sir, ' said Dale, who had been waiting patiently for his chance. 'He sold the car on Sunday. Probably needed the money for lodgings and the ferry ticket.'

'Well, he's still got too many options to get there tomorrow. Forget the local train, we need to catch him at Victoria or Newhaven. Dale, get his details to the Newhaven harbour master and Brighton police. Get another constable to help. Ask them to detain him, quietly if possible, until we can get there.'

'Yes, sir,' said Dale, and walked out of the room.

'We still have a problem, Bob, even if we can catch him. We have no real evidence, only conjecture. It's all circumstantial unless we can catch him in a lie, break his alibi or get a confession. Preferably all three,' Brookland added ruefully.

'Which means we have to bluff him into thinking we know exactly what happened that night, and that he is the only person who could have killed Miss Jenkins, and stolen the vase.' said Collins.

'I'm not sure we can. He'll know that if we had solid evidence we'd have charged him by now. We only have motive, and no other viable suspects. A good barrister could argue every one of our points away. No, Bob, we need to find another way to rattle him and get him to reveal information no one else could know. And speaking of unknown information, who were you speaking to in my office when I came in?'

Collins chuckled. 'Bracewell's editor telephoned you to see if you'd found him yet. Apparently, he still has his press pass with him, and his editor thought you should know. I thought it was best to confide in him that we need to question him urgently, and he offered help if we need it. I didn't tell him directly, and he didn't ask, but he probably assumes his missing reporter is our prime suspect.'

'I'm not sure what help he could offer,' said Brookland. 'I doubt Bracewell will contact him again, and an ad. in the 'personals' column is unlikely to draw him back.'

'No, sir,' Collins agreed. He fell silent for a few moments. Then a thought began to germinate in his mind. 'You remember our plans to fake a report that Jarman was out of business? Lure Bracewell back thinking he was out of debt again?'

Brookland nodded, 'Yes, of course. It wasn't a bad idea: it just had too many flaws to be overcome. We only gave up when we realised it would affect those who didn't know it was a ruse and still owed Jarman money. It would do more harm than good.'

'Right. But what if, on catching and arresting Bracewell, we give him a companion, a confidant? A detective from another division, playing a felon, in the adjoining cell? We could set up a fake identity, give the impression that this new man was our real suspect. They could be brought back together.' Collins watched his superior thinking over what he'd said. Finally, Brookland smiled.

'I think that idea of yours has merit. And I know just the man for the job.'

❖

Hugh Ross, dressed in a dark suit and soft hat, leaned his six-foot-plus frame against the door-jamb. His grey eyes took in the incident room and the two men seated at the table.

'Well, this place hasn't changed much,' he chuckled quietly. Both men at the table jumped at the sound of his voice and clambered to their feet. Brookland took fast steps to shake Ross' out-stretched hand in welcome.

'Hello, Hugh! It's good to see you again!'

'Hello, Joe. And you must be DS Mike Collins.'

Ross extended a hand to the other man.

'Hello, Mr Ross. I've heard good things about you, sir, mostly from the Chief Inspector here,' Collins enthused.

'No need for formality, Sergeant. I'm no longer on the job; please call me Hugh.'

'Call me Mike, Hugh.' Collins responded. 'So,

gentlemen, we have a fleeing murderer-come-thief, and scant evidence to present to the Judge, is that right?'

Brookland nodded. 'That's it exactly. We don't know where he is, or where he's been for the past few days, but he bought a ticket to Dieppe via the Brighton train, and we need to apprehend him before he leaves England. Plus, we need a confession or at least an admission of guilt; something a barrister can't easily quash.'

Ross had taken off his hat, placed it on the table, and was staring at the board in front of him as if memorising the identities of the man they represented. Brookland and Collins stood silently by, allowing Ross to absorb the images. His eyes roamed over the pictures of the victim, the crime scene and the other, innocent parties. Finally, he turned back to the two policemen.

'You're sure this Bracewell/MacDonald chap is the one who killed your elderly lady and stole the vase?' Ross looked Brookland in the eye as he spoke.

'Yes, we are.' Brookland confirmed, holding Ross' gaze.

'Why?'

Brookland pointed to the board and to their notes. 'He knew the old lady had money. He collected his girlfriend a few times, drove her home. He needed money to pay off gambling debts. He's the right size and build to get in through the pantry window. He lied about his whereabouts that weekend, and he retained a motorcycle for longer than his assignment required. His father is a fence, recently released from prison. There are other points that are circumstantial or coincidence, but that's the gist of it. The major problem is his alibi.'

'How so?' Ross queried. 'His old friend, from whom he borrowed the motorcycle, says he was home that night. He was in the house until morning, apparently. Do you think the witness is covering for him?'

'No, but he was otherwise occupied that night, so may not have heard the front door open. We simply don't know.'

'Otherwise occupied?' queried Ross.

'He had a girl with him. She arrived later, but she saw Bracewell briefly. She thought he was still in the flat too.'

'So weak alibi at best,' said Ross, 'but even if he did leave, without the vase to tie it to him, you only have speculation about his involvement and his slightly strange behaviour over the past couple of weeks.'

'And a good barrister will tear the case to shreds. That's if we even get to court.' Brookland sighed. 'That's why we really need him to confess. What do you think?'

Ross rubbed a hand over his face but remained silent. He sat down in a chair and perused the report of the crime scene. Then he picked up the witness statements and read through those. Brookland signalled to Collins, and the two left Ross to his own devices. They headed to the station's small kitchen and Brookland filled the kettle, setting it on the hob. Then he rounded up two cups and saucers, measured tea into the teapot and set the biscuit tin in front of Collins, who had seated himself at one end of the table.

'He'll be a while yet; that's why I brought you out of the room to let him read through our files.' He added the now-boiled water to the teapot and set it on the stand in front of them. Collins picked up the milk bottle, sniffed it, and poured milk into both cups. He set the bottle down on the table beside the teapot.

'What made him resign, sir? I heard he had a good record, was well respected. Why did he quit?' Collins poured out the tea into both cups, set the teapot down and took one cup for himself.

'He was all of those things and more. A fine detective, one of the youngest on record. Then a series of cases with poor conviction rates sucked the enthusiasm right out of him, and one day he turned in his papers, set up his own practice away from the Met. I wasn't sure when I rang him that he'd agree to help; it's been a more than a year since we talked so I didn't know what to expect. I'm very glad he did agree, though; we can do with his help very badly. He had a way of getting suspects to open up to him.'

'Well, let's hope they still do,' said a voice behind him. 'Any tea left in that pot?'

'So, as I see it, Bracewell is the son of an old lag, screwsman, fence, well-connected with the underworld,' said Ross, crossing to the table. 'But he's been away from that life for years, apparently honest and respectable, but has a gambling habit which he can't quit. Now he's in debt to someone he daren't cross, so he's getting desperate. And being desperate, he's making mistakes, making things worse. He needs a way out, and I need to give him one. One that sounds easy and fixes his financial problem without getting his body mangled by Jarman's bruiser.'

'And gets him to confess what he's done. That's the bit I care about,' said Brookland sharply.

'I agree,' said Ross, 'and I have an hour to do it, so I have to work fast, which means I have to make him open up of his own accord to get what he wants in return. Money.'

'And stop him from heading to France. It'll be much harder to get him back from there.'

'Yes. But that part I leave up to you. You have to arrest him at Brighton, with or without his confession.'

Brookland nodded. 'I'm sorry, Hugh, that so much is riding on your part in this.'

Ross shrugged. 'Par for the course. But I think I

have a way in.'

Brookland frowned. 'A way in? What do you mean?

'You say he's Joey MacDonald's son. Do you know who Joey is?' Ross asked.

'A small-time crook and dealer in stolen goods. Why?'

'Ever heard of Charles 'Wag' McDonald?'

'The leader of the Elephant Boys? Of course. Every London policeman has or met somebody who crossed paths with them. We all know about the fights with Sabini's gang. But Wag's long dead. Most of his gang too. What's the... oh, I see. But just because the name is similar, doesn't mean there's a connection.'

'But it doesn't mean there isn't a chance that they were related. And the small change of spelling could be an attempt to distance that side of the family. Or it could be an error on his birth certificate that was never noticed or corrected. I've known that to happen. I wondered if Bracewell knows something of those men and how they dominated the racecourses in past decades. He might know something of London's underworld today. He might even be persuaded to talk by one of them, or rather, someone he thinks is one of them.'

'That's a big leap, Hugh,' Brookland chuckled. 'Just who do you want him to believe you are, one of Wag's old associates?'

'Not quite. I want him to think I'm Billy Hill.'

Brookland and Collins both gasped.

'You're not serious! You'll never get away with that!' Brookland laughed.

Collins frowned, staring hard at Ross. 'You know, there is a resemblance,' he said as he circled Ross, who by now had drawn himself up to full height and hardened his features. 'And you're the right age. And with the trilby hat and smart clothes, well, it might work. But why would you be on the train alone? None of your boys will be with you - that wouldn't make sense.'

'Actually, you can help with that,' said Ross thoughtfully, and moved for the teapot to pour his tea. 'Send a few of your toughest, meanest-looking constables in plain clothes to hang around the station as if keeping an eye on the other travellers. Make sure they look like thugs so Bracewell doesn't suspect them. I'll come along at the last second and nod to them, then they can leave. That ought to allay his suspicions. Hill's known for looking after his mates, especially after leaving prison. Plus, his hatred of gang boss Jack Spot is well known. I figure he could be visiting someone in secret, doesn't want to be seen around London while he arranges something as a 'surprise' for Spot.'

Brookland rubbed the back of his neck. 'I suppose he could be taking a quick trip on the quiet. But how would MacDonald figure in his plans? He's hardly likely to be known to Hill!'

Ross nodded. 'I've thought of that. It will have to look like a coincidence, meeting Joey MacDonald's kid. Coincidences do happen, even on trains. I'm going to have to gamble that he hasn't any memory of childhood visits from gangsters. Something he can't disprove or wouldn't want to. I need to get him to trust me and confide in me, very quickly. I only have an hour or so, and if we're right about him, he'll be intrigued, hopeful. Let his guard down. He needs to think I'll look out for him. He doesn't know where his father is; I'll pretend I do. I'll give him the encouragement to join me. Just make sure the real Billy Hill doesn't get to hear about this!'

❖

Ross was still draining his teacup when Collins returned to his side. Ross had made a list for Collins and Brookland to peruse in turn, and Collins placed it on the table in front of Ross.

'Are you sure that's all you'll need?' Collins queried. 'It doesn't seem very convincing to me.'

That's because you know the whole story. Bracewell or MacDonald, whatever you call him, doesn't know what we're up to.'

'But he'll expect us to be looking for him eventually,' Collins countered,' so won't he be suspicious?'

'He'll be expecting a squad of police cars and fa-miliar faces: yours. He won't expect a middle-aged ex-con who's been his travelling companion since Victoria.'

'The journey only takes an hour or so. That's not long to gain his trust.'

'Even less to get him to incriminate himself. But he's not a hardened criminal, and he's out of his depth. Problem is, it will take time to get these things printed -' he waved a hand at the list - 'and that's the hard part.'

'We'll get those things printed today.' said Brookland confidently. 'We have a local printer who loves his work and doesn't have many claims on his time. He'll get this done tonight, I'm sure.' Brookland called for Dale and gave him Ross' list. He stood outside in the corridor for a few minutes to explain to Dale.

'Is there anything else about the case you need to know?' asked Collins.

'Yes,' said Ross, 'I think it might be helpful if you run through all that you know about Bracewell, from the beginning, in case there's something I've missed.'

'Right,' said Collins. 'Well, he's twenty-three years old, adopted as a child, but his real father is Joey MacDonald, screwsman and fence. Served a few terms, released recently. Was known to be living in Brighton. Young Hamish, or James

Bracewell as he's called now, is a journalist with a Wringford paper. He's the man friend of the deceased's nurse. He's known to gamble, owes money to bookie Trevor Jarman, was threatened by one of Jarman's boys at the White Oak pub. Spent a weekend on a borrowed motorcycle which belonged to the deceased's gardener's son, which is how his second identity came to our attention. Apparently, the son, Peter Miller, hadn't yet met Bracewell but did know a young Hamish MacDonald from their schooldays together in another part of the county. We checked everybody connected to the old lady; all had solid alibis which were checked out immediately, except for Bracewell. He disappeared to Hawford that weekend, apparently on assignment for his paper, so we didn't get to speak to him until a few days later. In the meantime, Peter Miller's motorcycle was borrowed by this old friend Hamish, not returned the next day, and so we were occupied looking for a possible new suspect.' Ross nodded, and Collins continued. 'However, he's the only one with motive, means and opportunity, plus he's the only one who's left town, or behaved strangely. And the second identity gives a possible background that makes him stand out as a suspect. There are no clues that point to outsiders; everything points to an inside job. Also, he's disappeared; everyone else is still going about their business. He staged an elaborate cover-up while he was supposedly on a simple assignment. He's our man, I'm sure of that.'

'I agree, said Ross. 'It certainly fits. Why did he reveal himself to young Miller?'

'We think his car got a puncture too late for him to change his plans, so he improvised. He probably thought being in two places under two identities would give him an alibi. He may not have realised Peter Miller's father was the gardener to his girlfriend's employer, or if he did, he probably thought he wouldn't be recognised by Miller Senior, anyway.'

'Well, when we catch him, we'll have our missing pieces.' Ross drained his cup and stared thoughtfully at the teapot.

CHAPTER TEN

Brookland had ensured that Ross' scenario played out just as he had suggested. Three of the station's most heavily built police constables found themselves in neat suits and hats, looking around the station platform as if watching for trouble. Several passengers skirted around them hurriedly, a piece of theatre adding helpfully to the effect Ross had hoped to create for Bracewell's benefit. Sure enough, a moment later, a slim man, dressed in a cheap suit and hat and carrying a small valise moved quickly past them, opened the door of a second-class carriage, climbed in, and shut the door behind him, giving a quick glance through the window as he did so. Other tardy passengers made their way along the platform, opened carriages, entering and closing them rapidly. One man waved to a woman still on the platform. A moment later, the guard stepped off the train and took a last look around for latecomers. As he blew his whistle, a tall, well-dressed man trotted hurriedly towards the second-class carriages, nodding to the watching 'lookouts' as he passed them. He also boarded and shut the door behind him with a smart click. The guard watched him, waved his flag and boarded the train once more.

By this time, the younger of the two men had found himself a seat in an empty carriage further along the train. He had watched the cluster of men on the platform with great curiosity. They neither boarded nor spoke to any passenger. Perhaps they were fellow journalists, waiting for a subject; they seemed resolute, imposing, even commanding. If this was how London reporters were, he might think of joining them. He could learn a lot from them. He saw them nod to another man, sharply dressed in a dark suit and fedora, with a raincoat over his arm and a newspaper in his hand. Another colleague, perhaps. No, wait. Their boss, perhaps. The owner of the newspaper, more likely. Yes, that must be it. The guard had recognised and waited for him! A press baron, perhaps! The young man smiled to himself. Perhaps this was his lucky day after all! He had managed to buy a ticket for the ferry to France and had planned to hide somewhere for a few months. It had been a while since he had been in France; not since his late teens, but nothing much changed over there. He could hide for a while, come back when the heat was off in a few weeks, try again to find his father. Or perhaps hide in plain sight, a new job, another identity as a London journalist this time. The money would be better, he was sure. Perhaps he could strike up a conversation with the man in the smart suit, see if his deductions were correct. Impress him, hopefully, into offering a job. He wouldn't expect too much at first, would expect to prove himself. Start at the bottom again. Not that he was far from the bottom now. Well, he would have to do it. It would be difficult to show what he'd done, though; he couldn't use his adopted name now, so he couldn't show what he'd written. Then it hit him. He couldn't get references either. That did it. He would have to think very carefully about his excuses. Something that sounded commonplace, nothing to arouse suspicion. He slumped back against the seat in a less cheerful mood than a moment ago and began to think through a new background for himself.

While he was lost in his musings, he heard the whistle and watched the well-dressed man moving fast to enter the train. He reminded the young man of a film star enacting a role; hurrying to avoid detection by the watchful guardians of the law. Or a cohort of fifth-columnists bent on reshaping the world. His mood gradually improved as his imagination took hold. Perhaps the sharp-dresser was not a Newspaper Magnate after all; the paper he carried not one of his own. Perhaps he was a member of the government, a senior diplomat on a secret mission to France. That still fitted with the men on the platform. They were there to see he wasn't followed. Perhaps one of them got on the train too; he couldn't see the end of the train. He'd have to look later. He was sure he'd recognise them again. They were tough-looking, as if they'd seen things. Perhaps ex-soldiers? He could remember men like that from his National Service days; men who wouldn't back down from a fight, got the best that was around, from the best food to the best bunks, just because they intimidated the weedier chaps like himself. Nobody did anything about it; the law of the jungle, they said. The survival of the fittest. Luckily, they had a use for him as stores clerk, so he hadn't done too badly in the end. All the same, he had moved away as soon as he was demobbed, just in case they found him in civvy street. He had moved from one area to the next, trying out temporary posts in different towns as he saw advertisements for minor jobs. Wringford had been the best town yet. And he'd screwed that up for good, the whole county too. Maybe even the country. He really needed to think up a good cover story while in France.

Ross, meanwhile, in his classy best suit (a present from a grateful East End tailor for the recovery of some very personal items) was watching ahead for any sight of Bracewell. One of the plain-clothed constables nodded and quietly said, 'he's just up ahead' as Ross walked past and nodded in acknowledgement. He had seen Bracewell enter the carriage further up the train and adjusted his pace a fraction to be sure of a last-minute entry himself. He wanted the choice of carriage to look forced and hoped there were no other passengers near Bracewell. He wanted the young man's attention on him, not on a pretty young woman or a disapproving matriarch or a garrulous salesman. Ross saw the guard dismount and heard the whistle so he forced his pace to enter the nearest carriage door. As he pulled himself into the train, he noticed one of the plain-clothed constables haul himself into the guard's van as arranged. Ross moved slowly down the corridor, glancing briefly into occupied compartments as if in search of a vacant one. The train wasn't full at this time, and Ross hoped his quarry wanted privacy. He needn't have worried; as it turned out, Bracewell was apparently of the same mind. Ross moved past carriages containing couples, two women with children, businessmen reading newspapers, even a few soldiers laughing and smoking. One watched him as he passed on down the train. He continued to move slowly down the corridor, looking for Bracewell in each corridor. Having recognised him from the photograph provided for just that purpose, and noting with relief that he was the sole occupant of the compartment, Ross pulled open the compartment door.

The man in question looked up as he entered and Ross saw the fleeting shadow of surprise across the young man's face, rapidly replaced with a cautious smile.

'Afternoon,' Ross said gruffly, falling into his 'cover' identity of a dodgy businessman.

'Afternoon,' said the other man politely, and returned to the book he'd been reading. Red hearts on a dark grey background; a romance by its jacket, Ross thought. Then he read the author's name and his pulse quickened. He seated himself opposite the younger man, unfolded his newspaper to the racing pages and said nothing more for several minutes. He wanted his quarry to relax and observe him in turn. He briefly lifted his eyes to the small leather case sitting in the net rack overhead across from him, then looked back to his paper. His companion appeared to be reading, but hadn't turned a page in several minutes. Ross decided to make his opening gambit.

'That book any good?' Ross growled in a Cockney accent, indicating the book in Bracewell's hand. Bracewell startled when he heard Ross speak and looked up in surprise.

'Not bad. Bit far-fetched, though,' he recovered himself and replied.

'What's it abaht?'

'A British spy, trying to take down a violent criminal organisation by challenging the organisation's banker to a high-stakes game of baccarat.'

'Baccarat? That's a funny way to take out an enemy. Why doesn't he just shoot him?'

'I don't know. International politics, I suppose. He's under orders from his boss.'

'Ah, that could explain it. Disgrace the man, perhaps. Still, this organisation could find somebody else to bankroll them, couldn't they?'

'I suppose so.'

''Course they could. Plenty of money abaht if you know where to look.'

Bracewell visibly started at this statement. 'I suppose... I mean, well rich people like to gamble, don't they?'

Ross laughed. 'Yeah, that they do. I've seen 'em drop thousands of pahnds in one night.'

'Oh,' said Bracewell, 'are you a gambler, then?'

'You could say that, son. But mostly I run gaming clubs. How about you? Waddya do?'

'I'm a reporter for a local paper.'

Ross smiled. 'Well, that's a good trade. Some of my chums are reporters. From the looks of you, it don't pay too well.'

'What do you mean?' Bracewell demanded.

'That suit's not exactly Savile Row, is it? But the tie looks top-drawer. You like your clothes smart. Same as me. Difference is, I can afford whatever I like.'

'So why are you in second class, not first?' Bracewell said snippily.

'Avoiding the nobs. Don't want to get spotted. And because I like to keep an eye out for... new talent, you might say.'

Bracewell was about to question Ross when

the conductor appeared and opened the carriage door.

'Tickets, please, gentlemen.'

Ross waited for the conductor to close the door behind him before glancing up to the case above Bracewell.

'So, business or pleasure?'

'What?' said Bracewell, startled at the question.

'This... trip. Business or pleasure?'

Bracewell opened and closed his mouth again, unnerved by the stranger's directness.

Bracewell made up his mind. 'Business. I need to transact some business.' Then he shut his mouth tightly, and crossed his arms, still watching Ross closely.

Ross shrugged. 'You're all set, then. You're not interested in a job.'

Bracewell relaxed, frowned and tilted his head slightly. 'What kind of job?'

'One that pays well.'

Bracewell hesitated. 'Doing what?'

Ross smiled.

'What you do best. Telling stories.'

Bracewell visibly paled. 'What do you mean?' He stared, wide-eyed at Ross.

'You journalists. You take the dry facts and make 'em sound interesting.' Ross watched him squirm.

'Oh,' said Bracewell, relaxing slightly and managing a small smile. 'I thought you were suggesting... something else.'

'I admire you blokes. It's a gift you have for words. A very useful gift.'

'Oh,' said Bracewell, then realised he was repeating himself out of nervousness. He was rapidly beginning to feel as if he were under scrutiny; as if back at school under the headmaster's stern gaze. He pulled himself together. He was a grown man and shouldn't be intimidated by a smart suit and a confident manner. After all, wasn't that just what he aspired to? He sat up straighter and tried to exude the confidence he didn't feel. "To feel brave, act as if we were brave," he had read somewhere.

'Well, thank you. But I'm really low down the journalistic scale. A cub reporter. I cover shows, local news, an occasional traffic accident, things like that.'

'How about murder?'

This time Bracewell looked ill. 'M-murder?'

Ross couldn't help feeling a little cruel at the way he was teasing Bracewell, but he was relishing his role and wanted Bracewell kept off-balance and uncomfortable for a while.

'A good reporter can make his name by covering a murder.' Ross continued as if he hadn't seen his quarry's reaction.

'I suppose,' Bracewell said hesitantly. Was he supposed to read something into that, or was he just jumpy? His companion carried on talking and Bracewell found his heart speeding up.

'Plenty of other chaps around, though? Like sharks circling.'

Bracewell nodded. 'There's always competition for a top story.'

'But if a good reporter got the inside scoop...' Ross watched his quarry carefully.

'Then his editor might take a chance on him from time to time.'

Ross nodded. 'Especially if someone did the editor a favour now and again.'

This time Bracewell frowned. Ross could almost hear the cogs turning in Bracewell's mind. He watched the young man struggling to decide if Ross was referring to him or a hypothetical situation.

'After all, it's not what you know, but who you know, ain't it?' Ross added. Bracewell appeared to decide Ross was talking in general terms and relaxed slightly.

'It's often helpful, yes, if you can get in on the ground floor, so to speak.'

Something stirred in Ross' mind, and he filed the thought away for later.

'So, if you happened to be put in the way of a good tip, you could put it to good use? Make people sit up and take notice, that sort of thing?'

'I'd like to think so. But where I live, that doesn't happen very often.'

'All the more reason to grab it with both hands when it does happen along, eh?'

Bracewell frowned, thinking fast. Isn't that exactly what he had done? Writing up his own murder investigation? Did this man read his mind? He couldn't know, really, could he?

Ross watched his man closely. He knew he had hit home with that last point. Time to take the pressure off.

'I know a couple of top-class reporters who got a break and knew how to push to get what they wanted. Knew what the public wants to know, asked the tough questions. They're enjoying the high life now, much respected and in demand. Practically write their own contracts. Good tables, good company, pick of assignments. Smart threads, nice flats.'

Bracewell was running his tongue around his lips; Ross knew he had the man hooked.

CHAPTER ELEVEN

Bracewell was uncomfortable with the way the conversation was going. This stranger was what he aspired to be: rich, confident and well-dressed. Probably influential too. So why is he on this train, and why now? He says he's a businessman, which could be true, but could also be disingenuous. Gambling clubs weren't exactly known for their honest practices; so, he'd be associating with gangsters as well as the upper classes. Well, he wouldn't be the first journalist to do that. And it wouldn't hurt to have connections, especially if his boss was looking out for him. Yes, that could work. He needed to fix things with Jarman; a cash payment would do that. He wondered for the umpteenth time if the Wringford police knew who killed the old lady. They must know he had disappeared by now. Eve would have reported him missing, his editor too. He felt guilty about running out on Eve. She would be worried about him, he knew that. She always worried about him. Worried that he was not happy, not eating enough, not content with his life. He had wanted to show her that he could be successful. Instead, he was a murderer and a fugitive. At least, he assumed that's what he was. Were they looking for him? Or did they have another suspect? Perhaps it wasn't such a good idea to bring the vase along, even if he knew his father could be trusted to unload it quietly. If he stayed away from Wringford, they'd eventually give up. The papers might say if the police had anyone else in mind. He ought to take a look at that newspaper to see if there was anything new. Unless it hadn't made the national papers. Well, if they were on to him, they'd trace his ticket to Brighton and then France. Perhaps to lose himself in London wouldn't be such a bad idea after all. At least until he knew what the situation was. Easier to find that out from London than France. Yes, that could work. Up until this moment, he'd been thinking in terms of staying out of the grip of one gangster, and now he was practically being offered a job with another. Well, it was better than being on the run. In fact, it was several times better.

Ross watched Bracewell as he sat quietly in his seat. Ross was a veteran interviewer and knew how to alter his technique to fit his suspect. In this case, a young man who was not quite a hardened criminal, but not exactly respectable either. He could go either way, and either way would suit Ross' purpose. In fact, he thought it unlikely Bracewell would have a clear understanding of the position he was in. He would most likely try to minimise the mistakes he'd made, especially since the police had not spoken to him since taking his initial statement. The small pieces in the paper attested to Bracewell's thinking: the police were looking for MacDonald and had only followed that trail. However, Bracewell came by his information, he didn't know that his car's movements and the meetings with Crusher were known to the police. He did not know the extent of the police investigation, and how much they knew of his movements. In all probability, he would regard himself as a free agent outside Wringford, unaware that the entire Metropolitan area was on the lookout for him, all the way to the coast. Brookland had arranged for the Brighton police to watch for him too; they, in turn, had sent a request to the French police at several ports, just in case Bracewell changed his mind again.

Ross decided he had waited long enough and spoke.

❖

'Well, do you think you have what it takes?'

'You mean my reporting.' Bracewell stated.

Ross smiled. 'Yes.'

'I'm still a junior reporter. A cub.'

'But you want to be the star.'

Bracewell frowned.

'The star reporter.' Ross corrected.

'Oh. Yes.' Bracewell's face relaxed. 'I do want to get on. Be a top reporter.'

Ross smirks inwardly. *The man is a gambler, a debtor, a thief and a murderer, and he thinks he still has a career in front of him? I must be a godsend to him. Good.*

'And you don't mind hard work or tough decisions?'

'Tough decisions?'

'Thinking on your feet. Deciding when to push, when to back off. Following orders, if you're told to stop. Learning from your colleagues. That sorta thing.'

'I can do that, yes.'

'Good,' said Ross. Then he watched Bracewell for a moment and said, 'I have a friend in the newspaper business in Fleet Street. He owes me a favour. He'll take you on. In return, you'll write a few pieces for me. As my publicity agent, as it were. All right?'

Bracewell nodded enthusiastically. 'That would be terrific, Mr?'

Ross smiled. 'Hill'

'Thank you. Mr Hill.'

'Thank you, Mr MacDonald.'

Bracewell went white. 'H-how do you know my name?'

Ross smiled broadly. 'Your face looked vaguely familiar, and as I watched you, I began to remember why. Your initials are on the case above you.

You have your father's nose, Hamish, and that furrow when you frown is his.'

'You know my father?' Bracewell gasps. Who is this man? He's certain he's never met him before, but then he hasn't seen any of his father's friends or associates for decades, so perhaps it's the truth. Unless he's actually one of Jarman's associates.

'I do. Or at least, I did. I haven't seen him for a while. How is he?'

'I don't know. I haven't seen him for years. He's been in prison...' Bracewell realised he'd slipped up. He sees 'Mr Hill' smile and knows he's been caught.

'You keep tabs on him, then. You plan to meet him, yes?'

Bracewell sighs. 'Yes.'

'Good man. Better not to lie to me. I might not feel so generous. And you need friends.'

'Yes.' Bracewell is becoming uncomfortable under Ross' scrutiny. He doesn't know what to make of this man. He is not sure if he should talk or keep quiet. He thinks he may no longer have a choice.

Ross has watched the man swallow and fidget. Bracewell is worried, but not about his crimes. That's good. He can work with that.

'Why are you looking for your father now? You don't want to know him as a father - you could have done that years ago. Is it for his connections or information you think he has?'

'Both.'

'Something illegal, I presume?'

'Yes.'

'Good. You want him to use his professional skills on something in that case.'

'Yes.' Bracewell was visibly sweating now. He felt like a beetle under a magnifying glass.

Ross settled back in his seat. 'I might be able to help with that.'

'Help?' Bracewell was puzzled. He'd all but confessed to having stolen goods and intent to fence them. What kind of help was this man offering?

'You need to get rid of hot merchandise for money.' Ross said bluntly.

'Yes.'

'I have connections. I can contact my people when we get to Brighton.'

Bracewell frowned. 'I'm not sure☐'

'You don't trust me.' Ross interrupted.

'I...'

'Why should you? You've never met Billy Hill before. If you had, you might think differently.'

Bracewell gasped. 'You're Billy Hill, the g...'

'Businessman. Or King of the Underworld, as you journalists like to call me. I rather like that.' Ross smirked, watching Bracewell's reactions. The man looked like he'd just met the Devil. Ross couldn't blame him for the feeling. He'd crossed paths with Hill years ago, and remembered the experience down to the last detail, including the supreme confidence that rolled off Hill at the time. It was that confidence that Ross was trying to exude now. From the shocked look on Bracewell's face, he had probably succeeded. Ross almost felt sorry for the man. Caught in circumstances caused by his own ambitions, unable to resist the lure of easy money, becoming a thief and a murderer to avoid discomfort and injury instead of seeking help. Even now thinking he would escape punishment and live well mere miles from the scene of his crimes.

Ross let a smirk play across his features as he watched the man in front of him. Playing cat-and-mouse wasn't his style, but it was useful. Bracewell had his guard down, caught between fear and ambition. Ross had a job to do, men counting on him to do it. The evidence Brookland had was largely circumstantial, and a good barrister could tear holes in it. In the worst-case scenario, it might even be thrown out by the court. It was imperative that Bracewell incriminate himself if they were to get a conviction. Ross had been down that path before; it was one reason why he quit the job despite a perfect record. He didn't miss the irony of the situation: he'd been asked to do as a private agent what he could no longer bring himself to do as an officer of the law. He'd thrown in the towel when he couldn't get the justice he wanted; now he was back voluntarily, once more trying to see justice done.

There had been one other concern in Ross' mind: Bracewell's profession. Ross had first-hand experience of the willingness of the press to look out for its fellows. Once other newspapermen took umbrage at one of their own being accused, they were perfectly placed to make life more difficult for police investigations. The tone and persistence of reporters could sway public opinion, create unwelcome publicity for the top brass to handle and highlight the shaky position the police were in. Brookland already had his superiors waiting impatiently for results; he didn't need the extra pressure of a hasty arrest on circumstantial evidence to blow up into front-page news for the major newspapers in turn.

While Ross pondered his own and his colleagues' positions, Bracewell appeared to be making up his mind. Ross didn't want Bracewell to continue with his original plan, to give him the chance to think things through, but he didn't want the man to get suspicious of his apparent good fortune either. There was only one way to keep a man loyal, and it was to think he had leverage over you, even in a small way. Just enough to bias logical thought in your favour.

So, Ross thought, this is where we test the rule.

CHAPTER TWELVE

'Well, MacDonald. Are you in or out?'

Ross' voice was harsh in contrast to his expression. Bracewell ran a hand over his face and swallowed. 'In.'

Ross grinned. 'Good. Though I thought you'd need more persuading than that.' At Bracewell's raised eyebrow he continued.

'A talented lad like yourself could soon earn his editor's trust. In twenty years, you'd likely be Editor yourself. No need to hurry in a quiet town.' Ross paused as if reading something on Bracewell's face. 'Or is there?' Ross peered intently at his companion, studying him. 'Are you in a hurry to get ahead, MacDonald, or just in a hurry to leave?' Seeing Bracewell flinch, he added, 'Hiding from someone perhaps?'

Ross watched Bracewell closely. 'Yes, that's it, isn't it? Someone's looking for you. Who is it? An angry husband, perhaps? Bill collectors? Bookies? Coppers?' Ross watched Bracewell's face as he rattled off one idea after another. He saw another telltale sign and stared at Bracewell as if daring him to lie.

'Bookie,' Bracewell reluctantly gave up after a pause. He felt the man's hard stare burn through him. 'I owe a local bookie £400. I can't pay up. So, I decided to... run.'

Ross pretended to think. 'Who's the bookie?'

'Trevor Jarman.'

Ross nodded. 'Not an easy man to reason with. But he'll listen to me.'

Bracewell visibly brightened at this statement. 'You could get him to back off? Give me time to pay?'

'I'll pay him off myself. It'll be my show of faith in you.'

Bracewell frowned. 'So, my debt gets transferred to you.'

'No, your debt gets paid, and the contract torn up.' Ross stated flatly.

Bracewell smiled slightly. 'But I'll still be in your debt.'

Ross shrugged. 'If it bothers you that much, pay me back out of your new wages. How does 30 quid a week sound?'

Bracewell's mouth fell open. 'Y-you mean it?' He gasped.

Ross nodded. 'Billy Hill don't go back on his word. But if you don't like the sound of it, feel free to run just like you planned.' Ross said curtly, pretending to feel slighted that his 'gift' had been taken as a hook. Even if it was just that. He picked up his newspaper and pretended to read one of the inside pages. He watched Bracewell from behind the paper as the man struggled to decide what to do. After a minute he let out a sharp hiss of annoyance and threw the paper down.

'Blast!' He spat out.

Bracewell jumped at the gesture and the exclamation. 'What is it?'

'Those idiots have gone and got themselves nicked. Blast them!'

Ross threw down the paper, got up, paced to the inner carriage door and back to the paper, picking it up and handing it to Bracewell. He took it, his eyes on Ross, and then looked down at the offending article. Ross had asked for this faked story to be placed into a specially produced copy of a national newspaper for just this purpose. He had gambled on the fact that Bracewell would be suspicious of any sudden good fortune coming from a stranger, and that in the event that Bracewell had never heard of Billy Hill or his men, the newspaper article would lend verisimilitude to Ross' cover identity and the 'offer' he would make. If Bracewell took the bait, the article would help to convince him; his own profession would reassure him and suggest a way to even the playing field between the two men. Ross was about to find out if he'd managed to get inside his opponent's head well enough to get him to trust his would-be mentor. Ross let out a breath slowly as Bracewell read the article. He could feel his heart hammering and his palms were sweating. Good; that would look convincing, hopefully. Ross walked to the window and stared out as if in thought, bringing his temper back under control.

Bracewell looked up warily as if trying to gauge what the article had imparted to the man across from him. He could tell that this powerful man was rattled by the news, but didn't really understand why. Men went to prison every day, he supposed. Then he remembered that Hill had been in prison once. Is that why he was so upset? Surely not. Were the people arrested friends? Was it their fate that was upsetting, or the business being conducted through them so important? Bracewell didn't think the former was likely; this man was obviously tough. It seemed unlikely prison held many terrors for him. He didn't say these were relatives, so it would be unlikely that he was worried about their experiences. That left money. The business that would go through these men's hands must be significant. That means there could be new connections to be made and fast. Bracewell already knew Hill needed to trust his people; he'd indicated as much. Well, he, Bracewell had connections of his own, if he could just reconnect with them after all this time. Perhaps if his father knew who was backing him, he might make himself known faster. The advertisement he'd placed in all the Brighton area newspapers had apparently borne fruit; he had received a response. He absent-mindedly touched the pocket of his jacket while he thought back to the ad. and the response:

'Young man, HM, wishes to communicate with his father, JM, at his earliest convenience at the Gaiety, Lewes Road, Brighton.' 'JM to HM. Brighton Station, 4.30 pm, 17th inst.'

Aware that he was wool-gathering, Bracewell cleared his throat and spoke. 'They were your... business partners?' Bracewell wasn't sure what to call a fence when he was speaking to a potential employer.

'Yeah, you could say that. Or you could say that the man who legitimises my dealings has just been raided and banged up by the coppers, along with his boys. That means they're after me through him.'

'Perhaps it was about something else...' Bracewell began, knowing it sounded lame, even to his ears.

Ross growled as if annoyed at the suggestion. 'Charlie didn't work for anybody else. In fact, he was mostly legit, at least upfront. Only a handful of people knew what he was. He mostly dealt in antiques for foreign buyers.'

'Perhaps one of his legitimate clients found out and shopped him?'

'More likely one of my enemies, and I have a pretty good idea who that might be. If I'm right, this changes things. I have to 'phone to my people when we get to Brighton, find out what the coppers know. I need to fix this problem fast, and I'll have to get back to town quicker than I expected. I need to mend fences with some of my former pals, call in a few favours. We'll have to put our business on hold for now. I may not have anything to offer you until I've sorted out a certain party. You don't need that sort of trouble.'

Bracewell said nothing, and Ross wondered if he'd oversold his case.

❖

Bracewell was aware that he had two choices. He'd been given the opportunity to bow out, so he could take it and return to his original plan: find his father, sell the vase and disappear across the continent. With nobody the wiser, he could have gone in any direction from Brighton. That would be the safe option. Stick to a simple plan, wait for the fuss to die down if he came back at all. Perhaps move around the Continent. It might be an interesting life.

On the other hand, he could take a chance, ride the coattails of one of the foremost underworld leaders of the century, and perhaps earn more than he had ever dreamed of. Perhaps he could follow in the footsteps of other investigative journalists, men such as Duncan Webb. Learn from them, become respected and admired in his turn. Hill liked him, so perhaps he could straighten things out, get him started again. He had the power, probably helped straighten things for others in the past. His connections extended to officers of the law so who knows what he could do...

'I might be able to help.'

At these words, Ross' heart leapt. He carefully schooled his face, looking straight at Bracewell, and said, 'Son, I can tell you've got a heart in you, but I don't think-'

'My father is a fence. He can help you.'

Ross allowed his face to relax into a smile. 'So he is. It's been a long time, though. Do you know where to find him?'

'I'm meeting him at Brighton station at 4.30 pm.'

Ross laughed and relaxed back into his seat. 'Well, well, well. Chip off the old block, eh? I knew I was right about you! I doubt your old Dad is as well connected as Charlie, but maybe it would be a good thing to bring in one of the old guard. That's if you think he'll be willing to come to work for me?'

'I don't know. I haven't seen him since I was a child. I was adopted when he went to prison, my mother having passed on. I've only recently been looking for him.'

Ross frowns. 'You don't know what he's been up

to all these years?'

'No.'

'But you do know he's still in the business?'

It's Bracewell's turn to frown. 'No, not exactly.'

'And what does that mean?' Ross glares at him.

'It means I've spoken to some of his former associates. He's dropped out of sight recently, since his last stretch in prison. They think he's putting his business back together. They've put the word out for me that I want to see him.' This latter was slightly disingenuous, as Bracewell didn't know who had left the ad. in the paper, but he wasn't going to tell the whole truth to this man and sound any more amateurish than he already had.

Ross folded his arms grumpily. 'Oh well, that's all right then.' He picked his newspaper up and opened it fully in front of his face, leaving Bracewell to wonder if he had just come across as a naïve boy trying to impress a rich uncle. He, too, settled back and tried to think how to redeem himself in the eyes of the gangland boss.

CHAPTER THIRTEEN

Ross watched Bracewell's feet from beneath his paper since that was all he could see of the man opposite. He needed time to think and wanted to make Bracewell sweat a little. It wouldn't do to appear too eager to take up the offer from a new acquaintance; nor would it look right if he ceded control to an outsider, and a youthful one at that. Ross would appear to take his time with the man, test his mettle.

Bracewell's feet were never still. They moved first one way, then the other, as if they were trying to lead their owner to the right decision. Ross fought back a smile. Bracewell's feet were like a metaphor for his life: being led first away, then towards crime, then away again. It didn't take much effort to guess the next decision would be in his favour.

Bracewell was agonising over his choices once more. Run. Stay. Flee. Fight. Fresh start. Success. Failure. Don't trust anyone. Quid pro quo. Make connections. Stay Away. Back and forth his mind ran, like a rat in a trap. Hill had reminded him he didn't know his father at all, save the man he knew as a small boy. That he, too, was an unknown quantity and may not be worthy of trust. Should he run to another country as he had originally planned, get far away and trust in his abilities to survive and prosper, or cast his lot in with an influential man like Billy Hill? Could he stay white when others around him were dirty? Could he use them and still come out ahead? In the end, he convinced himself that he might yet do both if he could build a reputation as well as a small fortune working for Hill. Others had managed to stay on the periphery of Hill's organisation, why shouldn't he? He would just have to be careful, stay honest enough to be excluded from the most obvious illegal activities, yet trusted to remain silent. Yes, that was it. He would remain on the sidelines, build a reputation for loyalty while being diplomatic and vague in print. Having settled his cognitive dissonance, he settled his body movements in a similar fashion.

As his feet ceased their tentative dance, finally growing still, Ross knew Bracewell had reached a decision. He relaxed still further, allowing his head to tip back so his vision under his hat now included more of his companion's body. Bracewell was still sitting upright, probably watching him in turn. Ross wasn't going to make it easy for him; in fact, he wanted the young man to work for his 'reward.' Bracewell was evidently ambitious and had shown himself willing to put in some effort to reach his goal, not entirely put off by chance or bad luck. Evidently, he had realised that things didn't fall in his lap and he had learned to plan for the outcome he wanted; his efforts to find his father while in the guise of a reporter on assignment, his apparent care over the robbery until it went so badly wrong. No, it was obvious the man expected to work for his advancement, at least until he found himself in a blind alley, and then he took the criminal's way out. A man like that would expect to have to impress his boss, so it would do no harm to indulge him by giving him all the time he could to come up with a few ideas on how to do just that. And Ross, as Hill, wanted to be impressed. Privately, he hoped Bracewell would surpass himself in that regard. To that end, he remained still, quiet and fixed on the articles he was reading. He was wondering how long to remain shielded behind his newspaper barrier when Bracewell broke the silence between them.

'You're disappointed.'

Bracewell's statement, when it came, startled Ross out of his brown study.

'What?' Ross jumped, recovering his character just in time. He dropped the paper and sat up straight in his seat.

'You're disappointed. In me.' Bracewell was leaning slightly forward now, both feet flat on the carriage floor as if bracing himself for an altercation.

Ross was bemused by the young man's change of posture but kept his facial expression as bland as he could.

'Not disappointed. I can't expect you to be a pro. You're nervy, but lack experience. You'll learn.'

'Yes,' admitted Bracewell. 'I will.' The determination in his voice was in complete contrast to his previous demeanour, and Ross sensed that his companion had made his decision and expected to be taken seriously.

'That's better,' He said neutrally. He once more picked up his discarded newspaper and unfolded it, this time to the sporting section. He held it slightly lower in his lap so as to study Bracewell once more.

He's hooked, thinks Ross to himself. He thinks he has his future ahead of him. Let him think he has what it takes so he commits to his next course of action. He wants money and respect. He thinks he has the talent to get them. I let him think that then when he offered up that plan, he proved he hadn't thought it through properly. I got angry. Probably that's happened to him before. Perhaps one time too many. Wonder if that's why he killed the old lady. His bluff didn't work. She saw through him and he silenced her. Well, I'm a little more of a match for him there. He won't be repeating that with me, and I want a confession, not another crime. So here goes.

Ross turned the page, waited a beat or two, and still behind the newspaper, calmly said.

'After all, it's not as if you have the police looking for you, is it? Then you'd really have to think on your feet.'

Ross watched the young man's own feet as he casually dropped this remark. There was a perceptible twitch across the carriage. Good, thought Ross. That went home. On hearing no response, he dropped his arms and the newspaper into his lap.

Bracewell had frozen as if he hadn't expected that line of questioning. Ross smiled amiably. Bracewell started to run a hesitant finger around the inside of his collar, realised what he was doing, and dropped his hands to his sides.

'I mean, a gambling debt is one thing. You can find money, one way or another. But you can't really know what it is to be on the wrong side of the law like I do. I don't think you want to either. Perhaps you'd better just let me sort out Jarman for you and go back home. We'll call it a favour for an old friend's son.'

Ross counted to himself. One, two, three...

'No!'

Ross pretended to look startled. 'No?'

Bracewell recovered himself. 'I mean, no thank you. I really do think I can help.' He pulled himself up in his seat and leaned forward. 'Look—'

His next words were suddenly interrupted by

the carriage door being pulled back sharply.

'Here, Bert, there's room in this one.'

❖

Both men looked up with shocked looks on their faces at the sudden interruption to their conversation.

A stout middle-aged woman in a red wool hat and olive coat was standing in the open doorway, gesturing into the carriage to persuade a stout middle-aged man in a dark green suit and flat cap to follow her inside.

Ross leapt to his feet and pulled his wallet out of his jacket pocket. He took out a card and flashed it at the woman. Bracewell also got to his feet, slower than the older man, but just as intimidating to the visitors.

'I'm sorry, Madam,' Ross said in a commanding tone and an upper-class accent. 'This carriage is reserved for us. Home Office business. You do understand?'

The woman opened her mouth to protest, but the man had finally arrived at the carriage door in time to overhear Ross' statement.'

'Come on, Deirdre. Leave the gentleman to themselves. Government business, didn't you hear? We'll look for another carriage up ahead, one not so full as the one we were in. You can have a window seat there.' He nodded knowingly at Ross and Bracewell, then steered the woman from the carriage and down the corridor.

Ross closed the door and sat down, putting his wallet away as he did so. Bracewell also sat down, but stared at Ross, frowning.

'What did you show her?' he asked suspiciously. 'Why did they obey you?'

'Business card.' He pulled his wallet out again and handed the card to Bracewell.

It read 'W. Hill' and the words 'Home Office' underneath. Above was the British coat of arms. It looked impressive, all gold lettering. Ross had arranged for a few variations from various organisations in case of emergency. Bracewell handed it back, obviously impressed.

'The trick is to speak as if you expect to be obeyed, maintain eye contact.' Ross confided. 'As I was about to say before we were interrupted. Thinking on your feet: planning, foresight and experience.

'Anticipating trouble and preparing for it.' Bracewell sounds as if he's reciting a lesson.

'And in my line of work, trouble is never far away. People want things from you, want what you've got. You need to keep control of things, show people who's boss. Sometimes you can make a deal, sometimes you need to teach people a lesson. Sometimes a simple threat. Sometimes violently. Not everybody is cut out for it.'

'And by that you mean me. You think I'm just

a cub reporter with no clue how the world really works. That I'll say the wrong thing or be a liability because I'm not savvy enough. You're wrong, Mr Hill. I am my father's son. And I can prove it.'

CHAPTER FOURTEEN

Ross held his breath and let it out slowly. Time was running out; he had perhaps twenty minutes before the train pulled in to Brighton station to get the information he needed out of Bracewell. He had the man's confidence; how far would it get him in the short time left? Should he encourage or deflect? If he appeared too eager, it would seem out of character with what he knew of Billy Hill. However, he wasn't Hill and needed to hear what Bracewell had to say. He needed the confession, as they had scant evidence of Bracewell's guilt. So, what did Bracewell need? The debt cancelled, to feel safe, and to feel he had a chance to make it big. He'd promised the first, assured of the third, but had he delivered on the second? Perhaps not. At least, not safe enough with 'Hill' for Bracewell to relax, let down his guard and confess to the man who could make it all go away. Time for the fatherly act. Ross cringed inside. Not his father, he reflected, remembering the Saturdays spent kicking a ball around a field near home, but perhaps Bracewell senior. Ross remembered that Bracewell's adoptive parents were both gone. Well, he was still on the young side, might still respond to coaxing from the older man. Let's see.

'Look, son. I get that you're ambitious. I get that you're in a scrape with Jarman. That's tough, but you could fix that. I'll help. I said that. You can dump your tomfoolery with me for now. I'll buy it off you. Then you can go home, pick up your life. Maybe all this will inspire you to write a book or something.'

Bracewell completely missed Ross' efforts to push him away; his attention being focussed entirely on the reference to the theft.

'Tomfoolery? Oh, no. It's not jewellery. It - it's a vase.'

Ross burst out laughing and then choked back his reaction. 'That's just priceless! No, not that. You've just proved my point. You're an amateur, boy. No wonder you can't get rid of the stuff. You wouldn't last two minutes with my lads. They'd never trust a screwsman who nicked arty stuff.' He sniggered and shook his head at the thought. 'Vase indeed.'

Bracewell opened his mouth, thought better of it and shut it again. He didn't have anything left to offer if this was the reaction he was going to get.

'How much?'

Bracewell glared at Ross but answered all the same. 'About £600.'

Ross raised an eyebrow. 'How d'you know that?

Read it in a book, I suppose.'

'I worked for an auction house. Under my real name. I learned a lot about antiques.'

Ross filed that information away and said, 'Well, maybe your old man can give you a job with him. It sounds like you're cut out for a fence, at least.'

'That's not what I want.'

'And what do you want?

'To be a great journalist. To write about crime, not commit it.'

Ross pretended to calm himself down again; the lad certainly was persistent, despite being dissuaded.

'Well, that's probably a safer bet. Hiding in the shadows isn't easy. It gets easier though once you make it big. Deals done here and there. Palms greased, a word in the right ear.'

Ross felt his pulse speed up again. 'You like the thrill of being around criminals? You like the lifestyle, the attention, the respect?

Bracewell nodded.

'You don't much like quiet towns. You want noise, action. Something to get the blood pumping, but without the risk of doing something criminal?'

'Yes,' said Bracewell.

'Your taste of petty theft didn't whet your appetite?'

Bracewell hesitated, not sure at this point whether to elaborate or not. Even though he was talking to a criminal, he still felt uncomfortable with what he'd had to do.

'No, not really,' he admitted.

Ross smiled. 'No. It's written all over your face. It's like I said. You're not cut out to be a thief. You don't have the nerve for it. I was right, what I said before. You should stick to the straight and narrow. You don't need the hassle. Go home.'

Bracewell leaned back into the corner of his seat. 'I can't,' he said.

'Why not? I said I'd square things away with Jarman. Oh. The vase? Don't tell me the coppers are after you for that?'

'I don't know. But they might be by now. I can't take the risk.'

'That's why you're running. Not just Jarman then.'

'No.'

Ross feigned contempt, although privately he felt some sympathy for the man; he'd dug himself in deeper while trying to extricate himself from his mistakes. However, he had killed a woman who deserved respect and care; Ross would do his job.

'So, if you have no taste for crime, why'd you do it? You said you were your father's son. You're not trying to tell me you think it's something in your blood? Or destiny? That's just rubbish!'

'No, I didn't mean that.' Bracewell pulled himself together and sat up a little straighter.

Ross waited to hear what Bracewell thought. 'What then?'

'I just meant... I saw an opportunity. And I took it. Then it all went wrong.'

❖

Ross said nothing for a few moments, letting the silence do his work for him, but watching Bracewell with distaste. Bracewell, in turn, was watching him cautiously.

Finally, Ross spoke.

'You mean you acted on impulse instead of planning. Didn't think the job through, plan the details carefully.'

'What plan? I thought I'd be in and out in fifteen minutes.'

'That's what they all say. Just means they didn't think it through. Next time think it through. Plan better.'

Bracewell laughed. 'That's your advice? Plan it better!'

'It's good advice. Learn from your mistakes. Check all your facts beforehand. Scope the building, watch the routes. Watch, wait, observe. Get to know the players. Don't rush a job.'

'What if there isn't time? What if you're in a hurry, need the money fast?'

'Then you're in the wrong game. That's why you failed. Poor planning. Like I said, stick to what you're good at.'

'And if you get caught?'

'Then you do your time and don't repeat your mistakes.'

Bracewell gave a hollow laugh. 'Somehow I don't think I'd get a second chance,' he said. You're right about me, but not the way you think. How ironic.'

Ross said nothing, but his mind was racing, and his heart sped up yet again. He tried to keep his voice level, school his face. 'Really.'

Bracewell leaned forward and nodded. 'You think I'm too green, not streetwise. You think I'm a risk, or poor fit for your, er... organisation. You think I'm out of my depth. That I'm a casual thief. That I couldn't cope with the realities of the criminal life. But what if I'm the one who's a danger? What if I were too hot even for you?'

Ross smirked but said nothing. This could be it, he thought to himself. 'Hot, boy?'

Bracewell nodded. 'I think the police may suspect me of theft.'

'You said that before. And I told you I'd fix it. It's not difficult. You can leave that up to me. As I said, I'll give you the money you need and talk to Jarman, tell him to lay off you. Just go straight, don't gamble again. Go back to your editor and apologise. All this will blow over quickly. I can make it go away.'

'Can you make a dead body go away too?'

❖

Ross stared at Bracewell. He had his fish, but would it stay in the net?

'A body,' Ross said, keeping his voice level. His eyes slowly lifted to the suitcase in the rack above Bracewell, as if expecting to see a disembodied arm swinging from the inside.

'You killed the bloke who owned the vase and dumped the body somewhere?' Ross asked with a frown as if trying to understand what Bracewell had meant.

'No, not exactly.' Bracewell said, all hesitation gone. 'The police have the body already. They just don't know what happened, or who did it. But I do.'

He's hedging, thought Ross, without taking his eyes off Bracewell. He doesn't know how I'll react if I'm for him or against him. And he hasn't actually said he did it.

'You killed someone?'

'Yes. I did.'

'That was stupid.' Ross impulsively snapped at him.

Bracewell nodded. 'Yes.'

'Did you leave anything behind, anything they could connect to you?

'I don't think so.'

'Then why do you think they'd suspect you?'

'Because I knew the person I killed. That's opportunity, isn't it?'

'Yes. And motive, if they've connected you to Jarman.'

'I don't see how. It's not like he'd volunteer that information.'

Ross smiled to himself. Bracewell evidently didn't know Crusher Evans had been identified, and by association, Trevor Jarman too. Another miscalculation in his thinking.

'Well, you're right about one thing,' said Ross.

'What's that?'

'This does change things.'

Bracewell looked as if he would speak, but remained silent and waited, a hangdog expression on his face. He felt like a schoolboy awaiting the headmaster's decision.

When no response was forthcoming, Bracewell continued. 'See, I told you. I'm too hot. That's why I ran. They were bound to figure it all out, eventually. It's ironic, really.'

'Ironic?' Queried Ross.

'Yes. Saying your men would not accept me.'

'Because you are an amateur.'

'Yes.'

'And you think they would if you'd killed someone.'

'Perhaps. Until they found out, anyway.'

Ross frowned. 'Found out what, exactly?'

"The person I killed.'

'Go on.'

'It was a woman. An old woman.'

Ross fixed Bracewell with an icy stare. His jaw clenched in anger. He already knew the details, but hearing Bracewell state it made it worse somehow.

'You killed an old woman for a vase to pay your gambling debts.' Ross spat out.

Bracewell shrank back. 'I didn't intend to. I didn't expect her to hear. I thought she was asleep upstairs.'

Ross slumped back into his seat and said nothing for a minute. When he finally spoke, it felt to Bracewell as if he was receiving a sentence from a judge.

'It seems to me you have two choices, Mac-Donald. You can run and hide, or you can admit what you've done. You need to make that decision by the time the train reaches Brighton.'

With that, he said nothing further and shut his eyes.

CHAPTER FIFTEEN

Ross gave a silent thank-you to Providence. He now had Bracewell's confession, so that would give Brookland and Collins their chance to build an airtight case against Bracewell. It meant they were on the right track all along; no need to look for other suspects. That would come as a relief to Brookland, Ross was sure; he knew his former colleague would be under pressure from the top brass to secure a conviction - there were few murders in Brookland's patch and that in the collective mind of the public and of the Chief Constable this somehow equated with a simpler task. Ross, like his colleagues, knew otherwise. Murder might be relatively rare, but that didn't make solving it any easier. With the best will in the world, it always took more time than anyone hoped. Waiting for medical reports, waiting for records to be checked, waiting to speak to witnesses and relatives— some of them hostile and all of them impatient. Ross knew that solving murders quickly was in part due to the location; how resources were allocated, manpower, pressure to solve crimes and training all played a part. This on top of the human reaction. Grief, shock, disbelief all vied for attention with outside interests: politics and money. This was something that Ross found unacceptable; all crime should be investigated thoroughly, recorded and presented before the courts for suitable sentencing. In his experience, this often failed to happen at some point; this combined with the bias shown by police officers themselves finally drove Ross from the job. But for all that, it hadn't driven him far; his private enquiry business was conducted only a few miles from the station, although he had not been back there for some years. Brookland had put business his way from time to time but this was the first time he had taken on anything quite so important, both to the town and to himself personally. Ross wondered how Nurse Gillespie would handle the news that her man friend was her employer's killer. Would she be shocked, or did she have her own suspicions now that she had time to consider the events of the past few days? How would she feel about him, knowing he was a murderer? Or was she still unaware that he was their suspect? He was wondering how they would break it to her when he realized Bracewell was talking to him.

'Mr Hill?'

'Billy, son. Just Billy.'

'Well, Billy..., I can tell you don't have a very good opinion of me now you know what I've done. But I would like to explain how it happened. I

didn't mean for anyone to get hurt, truly I didn't...'
Bracewell tailed off when Ross fixed him with an
unforgiving look. Ross dropped his eyes to the
floor for a moment and composed himself.

'Son, I've cut men to teach them a lesson. I've
had men beat up to teach them a lesson. I've or-
ganised robberies, fenced stolen goods and been
banged up inside. But I've never had to beat up old
ladies to get what I wanted. So yeah, I'm not liking
what I hear from you.' He drew a ragged breath and
paused for a moment. 'But I'll give you your chance
to explain.'

Bracewell nodded sadly. 'That's all I ask.' He
pulled himself up straight, took a deep breath and
started. 'You know I gambled on the horses and in-
curred debt.'

Ross nodded. 'And you borrowed from the
wrong person.' 'Yes. I tried to get an advance on
my wages, but my editor wouldn't let me have it.
I asked for more assignments, but I only got the
extra work after my debt was transferred to Jarman.'

'And then Jarman increased the debt?'

'He doubled it.'

'How did you fall in with Jarman?' Ross asked,
realizing that the answer might be important.

'The bookie I owed must have told him. An
envelope addressed to me and containing one of
his business cards was put through my landlord's

letterbox.'

Ross nodded. 'Nice touch. What did you do next?'

'I asked for more time to pay. He refused. Said it was out of hands now. He'd been paid off by Jarman.'

'Who's the bookie?'

'Man named Fred. I don't know his surname. He used to hang around the *Gazette* office on Fridays and Tuesdays.'

'How often did you win?'

'Once now and again, then a little more, then less and less. By that time, I owed him more than two month's wages. I'd stopped betting by then - the shock brought me to my senses - but I was getting worried about the danger I would be in if I didn't pay up.'

Suddenly, the carriage door was pulled open with a sharp tug. Both men jerked upright in alarm: Ross' heart rate sped up at the second interruption in their conversation. However, this time the interruption was from the uniformed conductor.

'Tickets, please, gentlemen.' Both passengers visibly calmed, reached into pockets and handed over their tickets. The conductor took the proffered tickets, punched and returned them.

'Brighton next stop,' he said. 'Five minutes.' Then he stepped back out and closed the door.

❖

Bracewell sighed and rose, excusing himself to head for the lavatory. Ross followed after a moment and entered another lavatory. He pulled down the window for some fresh air, even though he knew he should return quickly to watch his quarry. After a moment he returned the window to its locked position and opened the door, closing it quickly to avoid hitting another passenger.

On returning to the carriage, he found Bracewell had fetched down his case and was sitting with it on his lap. He looked once more like a schoolboy awaiting his punishment at the hands of his headmaster. For a fleeting moment, Ross felt sorry for him. Then it was gone, and he was once more the underworld boss. Neither man spoke for the remaining minute as the train pulled into the station. Ross was loath to say anything encouraging at this point since it felt cruel to offer any hope to the man sitting silently in his seat opposite, but he remembered that there was one thing he still needed to know.

'You still planning to find your old man?' Ross broke the silence to ask.

'Yes,' Bracewell nodded. I don't think he can help me, but I would like to talk to him again, after so many years apart. He's still my father.'

'Well, I can understand that. Blood being thicker than water, as they say.'

Bracewell laughed. 'Perhaps. It just seemed to

me to be the right thing to do.'

Ross smiled thinly at this incongruous statement and looked out of the window at the people waiting on the platform ahead.

The train came to a halt at the far end of the station, and Ross continued to watch the passersby rather than engage Bracewell in further conversation. He must have looked a little too long because Bracewell spoke again.

'Are you meeting someone here?'

'Yes. I have friends who will pick me up in their car.' Then as an afterthought, he added, 'Can I give you a lift?'

'Thank you. A ride into town would be good.'

'Not a problem. I'll ask my friends to drive you wherever you need to go.'

But not where you want to go, I think thought Ross to himself.

Ross opened the carriage door and held it for Bracewell to go through. Bracewell headed for the nearest outside door and pulled it open. He stepped down onto the platform, closely followed by Ross.

As he drew alongside Bracewell, Ross asked,' What do you plan to do after you've seen your father? Will you head for France as you planned?'

'Might as well. I've got the ticket for the ferry.'

'Well, good luck to you. I'm sorry things

couldn't have worked out between us.'

'So am I. I would have liked to have learned first-hand from the top journalists in town. And it would have been nice to have the inside scoop on how the upper-class lives. It's not so interesting out in the sticks.'

Your life is going to get more interesting soon, my lad thought Ross. Instead, he said, 'If we'd met a few months ago, that could very well have been your future.'

Bracewell nodded. 'I know that now. It's always easier in hindsight; I should have curbed my bets much sooner and looked for a better way to pay them off. Working three jobs wasn't as lucrative as I'd hoped.'

'Three?' asked Ross. He'd forgotten about Bracewell's other jobs for the moment.

'Yes, I had a part-time job as a porter in a hotel, and another occasional job with an auction house. That's what gave me the idea to take the vase.'

'You had an eye for the right stuff,' said Ross. 'Pity you didn't just bluff the old girl and run. Why didn't you?'

'I suppose I just panicked. It wasn't as easy as I'd thought. I suppose I didn't think it through properly.'

'No, you didn't. That's what trips up most unsuccessful criminals. They don't plan things properly. They don't account for every possible thing that could happen. Such as being surprised by witnesses, or even colleagues. It's often the little things that trip them up. Something small like a careless word or—.' Ross stopped as he realised Bracewell was looking at something further ahead at the end of the platform.

As both men walked closer, Ross realised what it was, but he did not slow his pace. They walked side by side for a few yards, and Ross glanced to the side at a carriage window. He kept his attention on Bracewell, who was evidently lost in thought. Then he frowned and looked at Ross for a moment, gauging his reaction in turn.

'Billy, there is a policeman on the platform. Is he looking for you?'

'No, son,' said Ross. 'He's here for you.'

CHAPTER SIXTEEN

At this offhand remark, Bracewell faltered in his stride as they drew nearer the lone policeman who was standing outside the gate, gazing up the road at something in the distance. Bracewell wasn't sure if his companion was serious or trying to unnerve him.

Then the ticket collector standing at the gate took a step towards them.

'Tickets, Gentlemen?'

Ross handed his over, and Bracewell followed a little hesitantly. As he did so, the inattentive policeman suddenly moved inside the gate and snapped a handcuff onto Bracewell's outstretched wrist. Ross grabbed the case from Bracewell's left hand and the policeman snapped the cuff on Bracewell's other wrist, securing him.

At that moment, Brookland, Collins and Dale emerged from behind a wall.

Ross looked at Brookland and nodded, smiling. Brookland stepped up to Bracewell.

'James Bracewell, also known as Hamish Mac-

Donald, you are under arrest for the murder of Dora Jenkins, for breaking and entering and theft of property. You do not need to speak, but anything you say may be taken down and given in evidence.'

Bracewell, still in shock at the turn of events, looked from Brookland to Ross and back again.

'Billy? I don't understand.'

Ross turned to face Bracewell. 'I'm not Billy Hill. I'm Hugh Ross, private investigator. The police will be taking you back to Wringford for questioning.'

'N-not Billy Hill? You're not the gangland boss?'

'No.'

'Oh, God.' Bracewell slumped and meekly allowed himself to be helped into the waiting police car, seated between two constables. Ross followed Brookland and Collins into the second car. Dale got into the driver's seat. As soon as the car transporting Bracewell pulled out of the station grounds, Dale swung their vehicle out of the car park, acknowledging the wave of the driver of the accompanying local squad, now free to return to their own police station.

'So, Hugh,' said Brookland carefully. 'How did it go? Dale has told us only that you got your confession. We all saw Bracewell's reaction, so we know you had him fooled right enough. You'll both have to make a full statement when we get back to

Wringford, but I'd like to hear it from you.'

Dale turned his head slightly better to catch his superior's eye, and Brookland added, 'Yes, Constable, you can regale me afterwards.' Dale smiled and returned his attention to the road.

Ross smiled and began to explain how he had followed Bracewell into the carriage, arriving at the last moment to appear as if he were evading pursuit. He explained how he had slowly won Bracewell's trust by a mixture of insult and encouragement, allowing his quarry to imagine a better life as a reporter with inside access to a gang of rich criminals. Brookland nodded and occasionally interrupted to ask questions. Collins, seated up in front next to Dale, looked to him for confirmation. Unknown to their suspect, Dale had entered the carriage after Bracewell and had locked himself into the carriage behind, assisted by the conductor who had placed a 'Reserved' notice on the door to prevent Dale being disturbed. He had heard much of the conversation through the vents, having removed the grilles between compartments, and had attached a borrowed listening device better to hear the men converse. He now nodded his agreement throughout the narrative.

Ross then described the moment he and his quarry were interrupted by a couple seeking an empty compartment. Brookland and Collins laughed at the image Ross was creating; they knew things could have gone wrong at that point.

'She sounded like my old Aunt,' added Dale and the others laughed even louder.

❖

'Go on, Hugh, ' said Collins. 'How did Bracewell react?'

'Ironically, it was perfect timing. I was lecturing him very pompously on thinking on your feet. I pulled out one of those cards I had you make up for me. That impressed him even more than my improvisation, I think. Anyway, it impressed the couple, and they obediently departed. Where did they go, Constable?'

'Several carriages down. Joined another older couple, I believe. They were still talking when they got off the train.'

'Something to gossip about and bore everybody they meet, no doubt,' said Brookland. 'What happened next?'

'I kept encouraging him and then changing my mind again as if I was trying to warn him off. Of course, it didn't work, and I wasn't worried that it would. The carrot I'd dangled in front of him earlier was just too enticing. The man was all ambition and little grasp of the realities of associating with criminals. I made it sound interesting precisely because I was trying to put him off. I wanted him to be so keen to throw in his lot with me he'd confess what he'd done because he thought it was like a rite of passage. I'd kept telling him he didn't know what he was doing; in some ways, I was warning him to watch what he said to me, but he took it to mean he wasn't my kind of criminal and confessed. I acted shocked and tore him off a strip; to be truthful, hearing him confess did shock me more than I had expected. And I didn't see the crime scene or the body, let alone actually know the old lady. She was a ballet dancer, Constable Dale tells me.'

'Yes,' said Collins. 'Quite well known in her day, apparently.'

Ross nodded. 'It's ironic that Bracewell chose to steal from her. If he'd been any good as a journalist, he could have written a series of articles on her, helped her write her memoir, that sort of thing. It might have brought in the money he needed to pay off his debts and get him a better job.'

'It might,' said Brookland. 'But you and I know that the type of people we meet in this job are often the ones who think in straight lines.'

'And some of them wear a uniform with crowns and pips,' said Ross snidely.

'That they do,' sighed Brookland. He wasn't looking forward to the paperwork to come; he knew how his superiors disliked unorthodox methods of detection. Most were plodding types with social connections rather than innovative thinkers. He knew he would come in for criticism for choosing to handle the investigation as he had done, but he wanted to ensure a smart barrister didn't undermine their case by putting doubts in the minds of the jury. Miss Jenkins' death deserved a secure conviction, and Brookland was determined to get one. Lost in his thoughts, he was vaguely aware Ross was talking again.

❖

'What?' asked Brookland, realising he was being addressed.

'Something wrong, Joe? I asked you twice if Bracewell's lady friend has been informed he was our suspect.'

'Sorry, Hugh, I was thinking about making the case for the Crown. No, I haven't said anything yet, but I will ask her to come to the station tomorrow. She may want to see the prisoner at some point.'

Ross nodded. 'It's going to be difficult for her, that's for certain.'

'Yes, it is. It will be a shock, I'm sure. She thinks he's a steady worker, reliable, supporting. She obviously knows nothing of his previous life or his gambling debts. It's going to be hard on her to realise what he did. She'll want to know why. The kind-hearted ones always want to know why.'

Lost in their thoughts, the two men fell silent for the rest of the journey. Collins had listened and watched them in the viewing mirror from his position up front. He too had wondered about Nurse Gillespie's reaction; he hoped he wasn't the one to tell her about Bracewell's actions. Privately, he wasn't certain he agreed with Brookland's psychology. He tried to put himself in the nurse's position. A man she liked and trusted had killed her employer and put her out of a job which suited her and took the life of someone she admired and respected. Collins knew that would make him very angry; would he want to talk to the guilty man? He thought not. But he had to acknowledge that the prisoner wasn't someone he associated with and thought he knew, and he had been part of the investigation from the start, not one of the possible suspects. He decided he wasn't in a position to second-guess the lady's feelings under those circumstances. In any case, it was probably better to wait and see how things actually developed. They'd all be heavily involved in paperwork and arrangements in the coming days; things wouldn't be as calm once the press caught up with today's events. Better take a moment while you could. Collins leaned back in his seat, folded his arms and closed his eyes.

It had been early evening when the two cars arrived back at the police station; Bracewell was charged under his adopted name and locked in a cell. Brookland had spent almost an hour on the telephone to the Chief Superintendent to update him on the arrest and the fact that Ross had obtained a confession confirmed by a detective constable. Then he and his colleagues set about writing up their statements. Dale was sent home straight after with Brookland's commendations ringing in his ears and a pat on the back from Ross.

Around nine-thirty that evening, the three remaining men met up in Brookland's office for a quiet celebratory whiskey. The mood, however, was far from merry; the three men were tired from the day's events and the build-up to it in the previous days. Ross had borne the brunt of the effort that day, coming in late and with everything riding on the outcome. Each man had then relived the day in their statements and was hoping for a good night's rest before the next day brought a fresh round of paperwork and procedure.

'You know, now we have Bracewell in a cell,' Ross stated, 'do we have any details that don't fit the sequence of events as we know them?'

Brookland shook his head. 'I can't think of anything offhand. Can you, Bob?'

'No, not that I can recall,' said Collins. We've assumed he took the biscuits - have all his pockets been searched?'

'Yes, all his clothes including the ones in his old flat,' said Brookland, 'but it's likely he just ate the biscuits on his way out and any crumbs fell outside in the garden. Not much chance of corroborating evidence there. He had the vase in his possession; it's being checked for other fingerprints but any others will likely belong to the members of the household. His shoes should match the prints in the garden, although they were too faint for a positive identification that will stand up in court.

I suggest we call it a day and get back in early to-morrow to interview Bracewell. If you two want to make some notes at home and bring them in tomorrow, we'll go over everything we think we have first thing. I'm not concerned Bracewell will give us a hard time, but a solicitor might, and I don't want to leave any loose ends that might give the defence something to pick at. I want our case to be as airtight as we can make it.'

The others nodded, got to their feet and said goodnight. Collins walked out of the door, leaving Ross, who had hung back. He turned in the doorway and said, 'Joe, for what it's worth, I think Bracewell will plead guilty no matter what his solicitor advises. He strikes me as a man who has bowed to the inevitable.'

Brookland rose also and picked up his hat and coat. 'I certainly hope you're right,' he said and followed Ross down the corridor and out of the main door.

As they reached their respective vehicles, Brookland stopped and turned.

'Hugh, I'm very grateful for your help today. I don't think any of us could have done what you did today. I hope you know what a good job you did.'

Ross smiled. 'It has been a long time since I've tried that, so I had a few doubts myself. Let's be grateful your boy was not a hardened criminal; I don't think it would have worked with an experienced man. But I'm heartened that you still have faith in me; your lads are a good team and I didn't want to let them or the old lady down.'

Brookland clapped him on the shoulder. 'You impressed them, and they didn't know you. I hope your usual clients appreciate you as much as we do.'

With that, Brookland opened the door of his car and climbed in. Ross watched him for a few seconds, then got into his own car and drove away.

After the two senior officers had left, Collins decided to give the day's events one last read-through before he too left the station. Collins had earlier made certain his young colleague knew how well he had done in his role as a silent witness. Dale had spent an uncomfortable hour in the next carriage ensuring they had a recording of the events as well as his own account. He had been congratulated by both Brookland and Ross in their way; Collins had felt it necessary to make it unanimous. He was cognizant of the fact that this was the second time Dale had shown his mettle; his out-of-hours undercover visit to the White Oak pub had shown Collins that the constable had initiative and the will to do a good job today had shown he was reliable. Collins fully intended to see Dale would be commended officially for his contributions to this case. He would also recommend Dale take the Sergeant's examination at some future time.

Collins looked up from his completed notes, filed them away in his drawer and took one last look at the faces on the wallboard. He knew them by heart, would probably never forget them, but he felt the need to acknowledge them once more. After checking the forms from the other officers were present, he closed and locked the drawer, returning the key to its usual place in the cabinet. Then he plucked his coat from the rack, throwing it over his shoulder and, placing his hat on his head, he too walked out of the station and headed for home.

CHAPTER SEVENTEEN

Just as Ross had predicted, Bracewell had informed his appointed counsel that he intended to plead guilty to the murder of Dora Jenkins. Now he sat with his solicitor facing Brookland and Collins across the interview room table. A uniformed police stenographer took their conversation down on her shorthand pad in a corner of the room.

Brookland gave his name, that of his colleague, and the names of the accused and his solicitor as present in the room. He also acknowledged the stenographer who gave no outward sign beyond a slight curve of an eyebrow. Brookland explained the charges, then continued, 'Mr James Bracewell, also known as Hamish MacDonald, you have indicated that you wish to give a statement in confession to the killing of Dora Jenkins following the theft of property from said Dora Jenkins. Is this still your intention?'

'Yes,' said Bracewell. 'It is.'

'Very well. Please tell us in your own words the events of the evening of Friday, the 5th of June 1953.'

Bracewell ran a hand through his hair and swallowed hard.

'I had arranged to collect Eve, Nurse Gillespie that is, from her employer's house and take her to the local for a drink. During the evening, a man named 'Crusher' Evans appeared in the pub. I was spooked because I owed his boss, Trevor Jarman, a tidy sum of money - £400 - and couldn't pay the fifty pounds I owed him that week. I pretended I hadn't noticed him and hoped he hadn't seen me. I got Eve out of the pub fast on the excuse that I was feeling tired. She didn't object; I drove her home, drove off towards my home, stopping to pick up cigarettes on the way. I had been turning the idea over and over in my head for days that if I could somehow get hold of one of the old lady's vases and sell it, I could pay off Jarman fast. I didn't think anyone would notice if I moved the items closer; there were so many in the case. Who would notice? I could shift the thing this weekend if I could rearrange my plans to be out of town, so I swapped assignments with a chap on the paper who was happy to stay in town. Then when Crusher appeared, I knew it had to be on for this weekend.

I stopped off in town for cigarettes and on the drive home, I realised something was wrong with a tyre, so I stopped the car to check—it had a slow puncture! I couldn't believe it. Of all the bad luck! I'm not much good with mechanical things, so changing tyres in the dark would be a challenge. Funny thing though, I had just passed a picture house and thought I recognised an old friend beside a motorcycle. I thought it was fate giving me a nudge! I'd met up with him a while back, after more than a decade since we knew each other as boys, but we didn't stay in touch. I knew he was a mechanic and would help me. Then a thought struck me: if he saw my car again, he would remember it. If anything went wrong, and I was seen breaking into the old lady's house, my car registration could be traced back to me! But if I borrowed his motorcycle, I could use him for an alibi if I needed one. Slowly, a plan began to form in my head as I walked away from my car, now parked around the corner out of sight. I walked up to him and feigned surprise at seeing him again. He seemed pleased to see me too. I talked to him for a while about this and that and admired his motorcycle. I asked if he'd be willing to loan it to me to get to work at the hotel the other end of town that night as my car was out of action until I could get it repaired; that I needed to get to work at midnight but the bus wasn't running. He said he could help, but I pretended I already had another mechanic to help me. He said he couldn't go home without the motorcycle or his parents would ask where it was. I suggested he tell them he would spend the weekend with me, stay over; I'd be back in the morning and we could catch up later. He asked me to take a note to his parents, drop it off on the way to work, so I agreed. Then he asked if he could bring a girl over that night, that she lived just a few streets away. I told him he could do what he liked since I would be at work and he agreed to let me have the motorcycle. We went back to my place, and he telephoned his girl, let her in when she arrived. I'd fetched all my gear out of my room while he was on the telephone in the hall since I'd packed for my assignment earlier that day. I left him my spare key and pretended to leave by the front door soon after she got there, as if going to work, but I stayed in the sitting room until well past midnight.'

'Wait a moment,' Collins interrupted. 'Even that late, you might have been seen leaving for the second time. Wasn't that a risk?'

'I climbed out of the downstairs window and got back in afterwards the same way. I used the side gate.'

'Oh. Go on, please.' Collins looked sheepish. That had not occurred to him. He caught Brookland's eye; his boss merely raised both eyebrows. He hadn't thought of that either.

'Anyway, I pushed the motorcycle for a bit before starting it. Then when I thought it was safe, I started it and rode it to Miss Jenkins' house. I parked it a bit further down, beside a hedge. I walked back to the house and crept around the back. I stood on the large rock and pushed at the pantry window to jiggle the broken catch loose, then I climbed in using the tree as a brace to get onto the window ledge.'

'How did you know the catch was broken and loose?' asked a puzzled Brookland. That hadn't been mentioned by anyone at the scene.

'Nurse Gillespie had mentioned it to Mr Miller. She thought he'd fixed it last week. I tried it: he hadn't. I wedged it again after I left.'

Brookland exchanged glances with Collins.

'You climbed into the pantry. What happened next?'

'I crept through to the living room, shining a small torch around to find the display case. I brought a small sack to put it in, and a sweater to wrap it up in. I got the vase out of the case, moved the other items a bit to cover the space, and wiped the dust with a handkerchief. I closed the case and then I heard a slight creaking sound. My heart began to hammer, and I realised the old lady was up. I hid behind the chair just as the door opened. I kept as still as I could, hoping she'd just leave. Then she switched the electric light on and the game was up.'

'You killed her to shut her up!' Collins burst out.

Brookland glared at him, but Collins said nothing further.

'Not like that,' said Bracewell. 'I mean, I didn't think about it. Beforehand. I just...' His hands dropped to his lap. 'Could I have a glass of water, please?'

Brookland looked at Collins, who got up and left the room.

Bracewell sat with his hands in his lap, staring at them, until Collins returned and set a glass on the table in front of him. Bracewell grasped it and drained a third of it before setting it back down.

❖

Bracewell licked his lips, drew in a deep breath and resumed his story.

'She came into the room, switched the light on. I was behind the chair, but she saw me and told me to come out. I had no choice but to stand up and step out into the room to face her.

'"You!" She said. "What are you doing in my house? How did you get in? Is Eve here?"'

'No, I'm alone.' I said. 'Then she saw I was holding the vase in my hand. She was furious.'

'"Thief! You came here to steal from me! Give me that vase, this instant," she said. "I'm calling the police!"'

'Please, no. I'm sorry. I just... I need money now. It can't wait. I need to pay someone...'

'"That's not my problem. And Eve doesn't need a young man who's a criminal."'

'I hesitated, and she marched up to me and tried to take the vase out of my hand. I wrestled it back and pushed her away. She staggered backwards into the other armchair and I was seized with panic when I realised she would report me to the police and tell Eve too. I was terrified and so I grabbed the cushion off the sofa and pressed it into her face. A few moments later she was dead. I stood there shaking for a while, my heart still hammering in my chest, but I thought perhaps everyone would assume it was heart failure. I was wearing gloves, so I knew I'd left no fingerprints. I replaced the cushion on the sofa, retraced my steps back to the pantry and after waiting a moment to calm down, climbed out of the window again. I wriggled it to shut the catch again and forced myself to walk slowly back to the motor-cycle. Then I went home.'

'You also helped yourself to biscuits in the pantry,' said Collins flatly.

'Yes. Eve made them. Is that what put you on to me?'

'One of the details, yes.' said Brookland. 'You said you rode the motorcycle home.' Brookland looked at Collins.

'Peter Miller says you didn't give his parents the note and hadn't yet returned home when he and the young lady woke up.' Collins stated.

'I forgot about the note until I found it in my coat pocket later that day. I slept downstairs and left again before they got up. I made sure I was seen leaving through the front door as if I'd been there all night. I picked up my bag, tied it to the motor-cycle and went on my assignment for the newspaper.'

'About that,' said Brookland. 'Why did you hare off all over the countryside if you thought you had an alibi? Was it to sell the vase? Why didn't you sell it, then?

Bracewell gave a laugh and dropped his head to his arms, now folded on the table. He straightened up after a moment and leaned back in his seat.

'I picked up the assignment for Hawford, swapped with a colleague who wanted to stay local this weekend. His kid's sick. He was glad to swap, and it gave me the chance to try to sell the vase. I had it all planned. Phoned an acquaintance who knew where my father was. Thought I'd keep it in the family, you might say. Well, I got his address, but when I phoned ahead, he wasn't there. Got a few tips, followed those up, still nothing. Finally, I came home, still had the vase. I hid it and returned the motorcycle after I got the car tyre fixed. I knew Miller would report it, but I didn't know how much he knew or would tell.'

'We got the whole story out of him,' said Collins, 'although only because he didn't want his father to hear it from us.'

Bracewell nodded. 'I felt bad about it, but it seemed like a good idea at the time.'

'And I suppose you couldn't borrow a vehicle from a colleague because then you'd have to give up the idea of the burglary. Which you nearly did until you saw Peter Miller.'

'Yes. I felt pulled in both directions at that point. And there were no trains I could take or buses that went where I needed to be. Plus, I was searching for my father.'

'Why did you quit your flat?' asked Brookland. Bracewell looked across at him in turn.

'Partly to throw you off the track, because I realised Peter would give you my address, and you'd realise it was me. My landlord wanted to fix a neighbour's flat, so I moved out. I knew you'd catch me if I didn't. I took the room in Jubilee Walk for a week. Plus, I didn't need the flat anymore.'

Brookland frowned. 'Why not?'

'I intended to run, so I rented a cheaper room on a weekly basis. By that time, I knew it was all up. Crusher found me again, and I knew I had to head to Brighton. I had been searching the newspaper morgue for anything about my father or his associates. I came across something which jogged a memory from the past. I read small adverts in the personal column and remembered how he worked when I was young. He would place innocuous short messages in the 'help wanted' or 'lost and found' section. He used a fake address or telephone number to indicate a meeting place. So, I placed one of my own in a national paper and my father replied. I was supposed to meet him, finally. Then I was going to head to France, disappear for good.'

❖

Brookland and Collins exchanged glances, and Brookland said, 'You left it until Wednesday to take the train to Brighton. Why was that?'

Bracewell laughed. 'I tried to get to the station on Sunday. There were police there. One noticed my car, so I decided to sell it. I tried again Monday, but there were police there again. I decided to try a travel agent, but could only get tickets if I travelled from Victoria Station. I got my tickets and laid low until Wednesday. No police there, so I made it onto the train. Now I know why there were no police in sight - you knew I'd spot uniforms so your men were in mufti. You could have caught me sooner if you'd done that before!

Brookland frowned. 'We didn't know you were missing until Monday morning and didn't send out constables until Tuesday. The uniforms at the station on Sunday were Transport Police, looking for thieves stealing from passengers. They weren't there for you. Probably they were there Monday too.'

Bracewell gave a short laugh. 'Wish I'd known that. Guilty conscience, I suppose.'

Collins leaned forward. 'You sold your car at the weekend. How did you get to London—bus?'

Bracewell nodded. 'I hitched to a bus stop further away, then caught a couple of buses into town. I stayed overnight in a cheap room. I really thought I was safe when I made it onto the Victoria train. I have to say, I never suspected a thing. I was completely fooled by that private detective. I really thought my luck was in, meeting Billy Hill like that. He had me fooled completely. You tell him from me, he's a good actor. He should be in pictures!'

Collins repressed a smile. He knew Ross was listening, probably laughing.

Bracewell seemed to have grown thoughtful. Then he looked straight at Brookland and asked bluntly, 'If I hadn't fallen for that trick, if I hadn't confessed, would you have been able to pin the killing on me?'

Brookland held his gaze for a moment. 'Honestly, I'm not sure. I've seen criminals walk free after barristers cast doubts in jurors' minds because a witness' statement sounded improbable. I've seen an accused woman fold under pressure on the stand when a child gave evidence. I've seen juries agree on less evidence and still others argue for hours over pages of expert testimony. We do what we can and hope for a conviction. But I will tell you something I'm sure of. Someone, somewhere always knows the truth. It's our job to find them and let them tell us what they know. In this case, it was you.'

Bracewell nodded.

'Why did you draw attention to yourself by approaching Peter Miller and risk his recognising you as Bracewell later?' asked Collins.

Bracewell nodded again. 'I bumped into him about a year ago and we met up for a while. Then I changed jobs. I hadn't thought about him for months until I saw John Miller a few weeks ago. I got quite a shock when I saw he was living in Lower Broadwood and was the old lady's gardener. I recognised him, but he and I had never actually met when I was a boy, so he didn't know me. At that point, I thought if I met up with Peter again, I would swear him to secrecy about my adoption and double life. Once I actually saw him, I decided I could probably pay him to keep quiet after I got the money and, much later, I decided I could also threaten to tell his father about the girl. But once the old lady was dead, I knew Peter would talk and you would eventually learn the truth. If I'd been thinking straight, I would have abandoned my plans the moment I recognised Peter's father. But I was scared of Jarman and Crusher, and all I could think of was paying them off.'

Collins continued. 'You rented the flat under your birth name. Why?'

Bracewell shrugged. 'I needed to do several jobs at the same time. Then when I got the newspaper job, I thought I'd use my adopted name with the paper and keep things legal.' He frowned and dropped his head. 'That didn't turn out so well, did it?'

'No,' said Collins. 'It didn't.' Bracewell slowly brought his head back up at Collins' remark.

'But why the double life?' Brookland persisted. 'Why keep swapping identities?'

Bracewell looked at him and said, 'I pulled a few tricks during my National Service, got into a fight with another man and we both ended up in a cell.' He looked up. 'I thought there might be bad feeling if I stayed put, so I moved around a bit, used my birth name instead. Then I got interested in journalism. I wrote a few pieces under my adopted name again, Ed Delaney liked them and hired me part-time. I needed to work at other jobs to pay my rent, so I went back to my birth name again, so as to keep a low profile if anyone checked. Thankfully, I was paid in cash, so it didn't make much difference. Then Ed gave me more assignments, so it was more difficult to do the other jobs. I had to give them up, even though I needed the money more than ever.'

'You wrote the articles on the murder,' said Brookland quietly.

'Yes. I'm not sure why I asked to do it. I suppose I hoped it would help if I could write it down.' He put his head in his hands. 'I still see her, you know, like that.'

Collins and Brookland looked at each other. Then Brookland had a thought.

'What about the house in Ivy Lane?'

Bracewell chuckled mirthlessly. 'Nothing to do with me. I noticed a 'J Bracewell' in the phone book and gave you that address. I doubt they're relatives; my adopted parents never mentioned family here. They died in a car accident in 1950, just before I got out of the Army.'

'Sorry about that; it must have been difficult.' Collins said.

Bracewell shrugged. 'They were good people, but a was a bit rebellious and never quite lived up to their standards of respectability. I'm glad they didn't see how poorly I let them down.' Bracewell stared at the floor again.

'Why did you keep the motorcycle until Wednesday?' Brookland asked. 'You had the car working once more.'

Bracewell looked up at him. 'I thought if I returned it immediately it would be obvious that MacDonald had returned, and you'd search for me again. I had to return it to Peter eventually, so I waited until I had found new lodgings.'

'You knew we were looking for MacDonald, even though you were in another county?' Collins queried.

'I didn't know at the time. I knew Peter would report the theft, but I assumed you'd be looking in Midfordshire. I didn't realise you'd tracked me over two counties until I got back to the office on Monday and they told me what they'd heard about the case. I was quite shaken; that's why I kept the motorcycle until Wednesday.'

'Where did you keep it, by the way?' Brookland asked.

'In the shed at the back of the *Gazette* office, with a cover over it. If anyone asked, I'd just say I'd borrowed it for a piece on motorcycle riders.'

Brookland and Collins exchanged looks. Searching the *Gazette* premises for stolen motorbikes never occurred to them.

Brookland then rose, and went to the door, calling for a constable. Stevens appeared; Brookland had him re-cuff Bracewell and return him to his cell. Bracewell went meekly. Brookland thanked the stenographer and asked her to prepare a statement for the prisoner to sign. When she had gone, Collins drew Brookland aside as they reached his office.

'No wonder we couldn't find a hospital that had employed MacDonald! Miller must have misheard him!'

Brookland nodded. 'I noticed that too. We'll have to chalk that one up to bad luck.' Then he gasped. 'He must have said "the Aspinall" and Miller thought he said "the hospital!"' He chuckled and shook his head. Collins groaned.

'Never mind. We got him, thanks to the leads we did get.'

At that moment, Ross reappeared, holding a tray of teacups and a plate of biscuits. He entered the office and put the tray down on Brookland's side table. Brookland and Collins made noises of appreciation and followed him inside, each picking up a cup and taking a biscuit.

'Hugh, this is the second time in two days you've anticipated our wishes,' laughed Brookland good-naturedly. Collins, his mouth full of biscuit, just nodded.

Ross beamed at them. 'It's nice to be appreciated,' he said. 'And I hope you still feel the same when you get my bill.'

❖

After Ross had left the station, Brookland disappeared into his office and shut the door. Collins wandered down to the cells to check on the prisoner, returning the greeting of the constable on duty.

'How is our prisoner, Bowers?'

'Very quiet,' replied the constable, a thickset, ginger-haired man in his mid-fifties. 'I gave him a mug of tea. He was very polite about it. I don't think he'll give us any trouble tonight.'

'You'll see he gets a meal later, and breakfast tomorrow before he's transferred to the Magistrates Court?

'Yes, Sergeant. We'll look after him. All according to proper procedure.'

'Good. Thank you. This needs to be by the book, but courteously.'

'You can rely on us. Do you want to be let into

the cell?'

'No, Bowers, I'll check on him from outside, thanks.'

'Very good, Sergeant.' He's in number three.'

Bowers smiled and opened the door to the cell-block. Collins slipped inside and slid aside the plate covering the small observation window to cell three. Bracewell was sitting on the bunk with his head in his hands. Collins slid the plate back and walked to the door, opened it and waited while Bowers relocked it.

'Goodnight, Bowers, and thanks,' he said as he walked away from the guard.

'Goodnight, Sergeant.'

❖

Collins headed back to the CID offices to talk with Brookland about their prisoner. Brookland, he knew, was trying to maintain an impartial attitude to their prisoner. To discharge his duty fairly, without prejudice. The phrase came unbidden into his head. Not an easy task when dealing with an impulsive, fatal act from one who had, until then, stayed mainly on the right side of the law. Collins, too, wanted the comfort of justice borne from fairness, but he felt a duty to the betrayed too. Bracewell had violated Eve's trust, as well as that of her employer. Collins couldn't help feeling angry at the futility of the young man's actions and the cruel ending of an elderly life, especially one who had given so much to others all her life. He had unloaded his conscience to Brookland. His boss had listened sympathetically to his young sergeant's voicing of his own thoughts vis-à-vis Bracewell's chain of actions. A stray thought came into Brookland's mind; he parked it for later examination.

'Bob, I agree with all that you say, but I don't want our actions on this case to be seen as anything but the requirement of the law. I have no grounds for making any recommendations beyond following procedure and advising against bail, should it be requested.'

Collins nodded. 'I suppose we'll have our answer tomorrow.'

Brookland nodded. 'You know, Bob, it's strange how this went. If Bracewell's tyre hadn't been punctured, he'd not have needed Miller's motorcycle. He'd have gone to Hawford and returned without his movements being tracked. We'd never have known about his second identity. He'd probably have made it to France.'

'He could have stopped gambling before it got the better of him.' Collins groused.

Brookland looked down his nose at Collins. 'Bob, it's not that simple when you're in the grip of a vice.'

Collins grunted and caught Brookland's eye. 'Oh, well, perhaps not. It's over now.'

Brookland smiled at his younger colleague. 'For

him, yes. Now go home and stop fretting.'

Collins laughed. 'Yes, sir. Goodnight.'

'Goodnight, Bob. 'I'll see you tomorrow.'

CHAPTER EIGHTEEN

"Charges brought in the murder of Dora Jenkins, 82

by *Wringford Gazette and Echo* reporter

A man was charged today in connection with
the murder of Dora Jenkins, aged 82, of Lower
Broadwood. James Bracewell, 23, appeared at
Wringford Magistrates Court to answer to the
charges put to him. There was no request for
bail."

-Evening edition, *Wringford Gazette and Echo*

Bracewell appeared first thing before the Magistrates dressed smartly in a dark blue suit. His solicitor accompanied him; Brookland, Collins and
Ross stood nearby.

Bracewell stood quietly as the charges were
read to him, and when asked by the clerk to respond to the charge, simply said, 'Guilty.'

Brookland and Collins quietly breathed a sigh
of relief; Eve Gillespie wiped a tear from her eyes
but remained silent.

The Justice directed the clerk to ensure that a guilty plea was entered in writing; this being done, the Justice informed Bracewell that the court did not have sufficient power to sentence him and that he would be sentenced at a later date. He consulted with the clerk for a few moments and informed Bracewell that the sentence would be handed down at the Assizes in six days' time.

Bracewell was taken into custody once more, accompanied by two officers of the court.

Brookland and Collins spoke briefly to Eve Gillespie before arranging for a constable to take her home. They returned to the police station after speaking to the court clerk for a few minutes, the rest of their day being occupied with matters unrelated to the Bracewell case.

Then, in the late afternoon, they had a visitor.

The station was quiet; officers still on patrol, no visitors to the station. A smartly dressed man with ever-alert eyes slipped quietly in through the back door and removed his hat as he stood by Brookland's open door. Brookland and Ross were discussing Bracewell's appearance that day, and both looked up at the sound of a cough. Both were on their feet in half a second.

Billy Hill laughed and held up a hand. 'Relax, Gents. This is a friendly visit. Just the three of us.' He opened his coat to show he was unarmed. He pointed to a chair. 'May I sit?'

Brookland waved a hand, and Hill brought the spare chair forward to the desk and sat down.

'I appreciate you fellas looking surprised,' he said, smiling pleasantly, and conversing in a pleasant drawl, 'but I heard about that little impersonation you did on the train, Mr Ross, and I wanted to tell you I'm not upset. Amused, actually. That was a pretty smart piece of police work.'

'Well, thank you, Mr Hill,' said Ross. 'And your reputation got us our killer and a confession. But I would like to know how you found out about it.'

'As would I,' said Brookland.

Hill shrugged. 'The conductor is married to my wife's hairdresser. He told her, she told my wife, who told me. So, I had one of my boys in court today.'

Brookland nodded. 'As easy as that.'

'As easy as that,' Hill acknowledged. 'You understand, I'm sure, that I had to check for myself, that my reputation was not, shall we say, misrepresented in any way? Good. I thought you should know, as a courtesy, that I am satisfied you were doing your jobs in the best way you could, under the circumstances, and I don't intend to interfere. So, I thought I'd just come around and offer my congratulations on getting your killer.'

Hill got to his feet; the others rose with him. 'Nice meeting you, Gents.'

'Er, likewise,' Ross responded, and Brookland nodded.

Hill vanished through the door and out into the corridor. Brookland and Ross followed quickly, opening the back door in time to see a black Austin Princess driving away.

Both let out a long breath.

Ross asked, 'Did that really happen? Did we just have a conversation with a gangster?'

Brookland nodded. 'Indeed, we did. But I don't think we're supposed to remember it.'

Ross stared at him for a beat, then nodded.

According to police procedure, it is not enough that a case has been investigated thoroughly and the guilty party arrested. It is equally important that the case be correctly prepared for court, with all pertinent facts stated in order and accompanied by witness testimony. The officer in charge of the case must see that those who are to prosecute it have all the necessary facts and may decide for themselves not only what is admissible as evidence but also anything which has a bearing on the case, such as the conduct of the parties involved. Hence the need for full disclosure in the form of written reports and statements.

The next few days would see Brookland mostly missing from the station to converse with his superiors, judges and other officials as Bracewell's case was forwarded for prosecution. Brookland wanted to be sure the young man's case was handled with some care: the elderly victim had been a minor celebrity in her heyday; Brookland intended to see that the respect for her death and the plight of her murderer were given equal weight in both court and public opinion. He was well aware of the likely outcome for Bracewell and didn't want Eve or Dora's nephew to be subjected to unpleasant talk if he could help it.

Collins and Dale pressed on with the paperwork to prepare the case for court. The witness statements were typed and signed by all parties present, the evidence clearly identified and correctly labelled. Brookland had passed the responsibility for the preparation to Collins, with the assurance that he would look over their efforts and add his own report for their attention.

'Bob,' Brookland had said, 'I'm going to talk with the Chief Superintendent about Bracewell. I want him to have a fair shake in this trial, but I don't want the sympathy to be entirely with him. He killed a defenceless old lady for personal gain, and she deserves justice. I'm relying on you to put our case together and see that there are no slip-ups with the evidence or statements. Bracewell may plead guilty or he may panic and change his mind. I want us to be ready if that happens.'

Collins had nodded. 'I feel the same way, sir. Don't worry, we'll see this is wrapped up tightly.'

Brookland had removed himself, satisfied his people would do their best to see the elderly victim's case would have their best attention in the next few days. The two men then worked their way through the ensuing paperwork, diligently filling out forms and paying attention to every detail, clearly setting out the facts and occurrences in full, without glossing over any of the action to ensure there were no questions that might arise thereafter. Collins was well aware that reports were often taken at face value, and he wanted no precipitous action taken due to inattention. He knew the wording had to be precise and show the suspect's intention throughout.

Nurse Gillespie had appeared in the afternoon; she requested to visit the accused, now in prison awaiting his day in court. Collins had Constable Stevens arrange this and to collect and drive her to the prison the following day.

Monday morning found Brookland back in his office, teacup in hand, reviewing reports and newspaper articles spread out on his desk. He read through all of the paperwork carefully, ensuring all the accounts were factual and true. He had dropped by each day to countersign his officers' paperwork and fill out his own senior officer's forms, setting them aside in his out-tray. He read through the newspaper articles that Collins and Dale had marked for him; in contrast to the reports, most articles had exaggerated the danger to the public from their suspect, and managed to imply that the police were slow to make an arrest; nothing new there. However, there were a few comments from colleagues which did paint a truer picture of Bracewell, and those, unsurprisingly, were from the *Wringford Gazette and Echo*. They included short accounts of the victim and her killer, with a footnote that the latter had not confided to anyone that he was in financial difficulties. It ended with a short polemic on gambling.

Other newspapers had been less kind. One lamented the behaviour of young men today, one suggested the old lady should have been less trusting and encouraged other elderly persons to be more circumspect in their dealings with unknown persons. One paper got most of the facts wrong, even misspelling the name of the victim, and hinted that the crime was mob-related. Brookland suspected the articles would become more antagonistic to all parties once the details found their way into the newspapers. He got up and took the signed papers through to Collins in the incident room.

'Here's the last of them, Bob,' he said as he put the sheets on the table. 'Where are we with the ones for the court?'

'Just finished typing them an hour ago,' he indicated the stack in the tray in front of him.

'Good. I'll take them all and countersign them. Then you can get them sent over unless you want to go yourself?'

'I'll send Stevens. He can charm the lady clerk into filing them today.'

Brookland raised an eyebrow. 'Do I detect a story?'

'Only that he appears to have an admirer in the form of a young secretary there.'

'Well, I wouldn't want to stand in the way of young love,' Brookland chuckled. Then his face fell. 'Talking of youth, how is our young nurse these days? You said she'd seen Bracewell? How did she seem?'

Collins opened his mouth to speak, but another voice beat him to it.

'I came to talk to you about that,' a familiar female voice stated quietly.

The two men turned to see Eve Gillespie standing in the doorway. Michael Dale stood behind her, silently apologetic for their mistimed visit.

Brookland held out his hand in greeting, while Collins scrambled for another chair.

'Miss Gillespie, what can we do for you?' Brookland asked as they shook hands. 'Please, sit down.'

Eve Gillespie seated herself, placing her bag alongside her. 'As I'm sure you know, I saw James yesterday.'

Both men nodded, watching her attentively as she continued. 'I asked him why he did it-' she paused here and took a breath, '-and what he intends to do in court.'

Brookland watched her uncomfortably. He had his own opinion; he didn't want to burden her with that unless she asked. After a moment's pause, and when she realised he was waiting for her to speak, she continued.

'He said he'd had time to think about his actions. He felt he was trapped by his own past, but couldn't think outside of the choices he kept making. As if he could only ever see one path to take somehow. Tunnel vision, I think they call it. Once the pressure was off, he began to realise he could have taken decisions differently. Been a little more honest about his finances, and his gambling, and asked for help.'

Brookland nodded. 'They often do, when it's too late.'

Eve looked him in the eye and said, 'Perhaps I should have seen he was in some sort of difficulty sooner? Could I have done something differently?'

Collins started to protest, and Brookland shook his head, 'No, Miss Gillespie, none of it is your fault. He chose to keep it from you, lied to you and betrayed your trust. He's a grown man, and the fault lies squarely with him. You have nothing to blame yourself for, truly.'

Eve sighed and said, 'I do hope you're right, Chief Inspector. Indeed, he told me himself that he was sorry for the way he behaved, and for the trouble he brought me. He intends to plead guilty, as I'm sure you know. And he fully expects to hang for it.' She wiped her eyes with a handkerchief from her pocket.

Brookland had been wondering if Bracewell would stick to his plan; it appears he was, at least for now. Collins was offering his help with the press if she should be confronted by their curiosity and hopes of a scoop. Eve thanked him and said, 'I told him I would support him while he's in prison; but that I cannot condone what he did. He accepts that.' She rose from her seat, collected her handbag and said goodbye, walking calmly out of the room with Collins in tow. He returned a few minutes later.

'Sir, do you think Bracewell really will plead guilty?' he asked. Brookland shrugged.

'I hope so, it will make her life easier, but if he starts to think about what lies ahead for him, he may change his mind.'

'Well, our case is as airtight as we can make it, so there won't be much to question if it did go to trial, but I hope he does stick to his decision all the same.'

'Me too, Bob, me too.'

❖

Brookland returned to his office to think. He reflected on what he knew of Bracewell's past and the conversation with Eve Gillespie. He thought back to conversations with the people he had interviewed, colleagues present and past, and to Bracewell's conversations with Ross and himself. He reread the case statements once more and then reached for the newspaper clippings reporting on the investigation and its aftermath. Then he picked up the telephone, and, checking his contact book, dialled a little-used number. After a conversation lasting no more than sixteen minutes, he thanked the man he had called and hung up. Then he pulled a pad of paper towards himself, uncapped his pen and began to write.

Collins had also been thinking about the people involved in the investigation, and how it had affected them. Collins had walked back to his own desk in the incident room whilst reflecting on Eve's visit. He had seen from her slightly drooping posture that she was conflicted. He knew her to be sympathetic, but her training would have been exacted; no room for aberrant behaviour. People like that wanted explanations for impulsive and unlawful acts, but the duty of the police was to record the breach and bring the culprits to justice. They were not required to discover the psychology behind a crime. That was no part of the job. Privately, as a human being, Collins knew how she felt, and he raged inwardly at the effect of the crime on all those involved, not just the victim or the culprit. Finally, he decided to speak to Brookland and headed back out of the room again.

From his position near the still-open door to Brookland's office, Collins frowned as he listened to Brookland's side of the conversation. He hadn't meant to eavesdrop, but felt unable to move away or make his presence known. He heard Brookland replace the receiver and quickly reconsidered his decision to speak.

CHAPTER NINETEEN

"Assizes sentence for confessed murderer
by *Wringford Gazette and Echo* reporter

James Bracewell, aged 23, of Lower Broad-wood, having pleaded guilty to the charges of burglary, assault and murder of Dora Jenkins, aged 82, of Lower Broadwood, is to appear before the County Assize Court today."

- *Wringford Gazette and Echo*

Bracewell found himself in the County Court on the 6th of July to hear sentence passed on him by Judge Henry Westing.

He stood quietly, dressed in a dark suit, flanked by Brookland and Collins, and listened to the court clerk read the charges. When asked, he again confirmed his details and that he would plead guilty to the charges against him. Westing, a tall, handsome man of fifty-seven years, listened quietly and attentively to his clerk, his hands clasped lightly on the bench before him. He was the very picture of calm authority, his grey eyes shifting focus from his clerk to the DCI as he addressed Brookland.

'Detective Chief Inspector Brookland, what is the case for the Crown?'

Brookland began his summary of the case, reading slowly and carefully from his prepared notes. He took his time, describing the crime, the investigation into Bracewell, and Bracewell's actions up until the arrest at Brighton station. Then he looked to the Clerk of the Court who nodded, and he stood silently once more.

'Mr Selwood,' the Judge addresses Bracewell's barrister, 'do you wish to raise any points in mitigation of your client's actions?'

Selwood, a stoutish, pleasant-faced man in his early sixties, nodded and said, 'Yes, Your Honour, I do. My client is the product of a broken home, a young man who had to make his way in the world without the guiding influence of a responsible father. Indeed, his father is a convicted felon. My client has managed to hold down jobs, becoming a junior reporter for the *Wringford Gazette and Echo*. It was only when the temptation of gambling to improve his finances came his way that he departed from his previously upright good character and sought to put an end to his debts by means of theft since he concluded that he could not come by the money honestly. That money was needed urgently to prevent physical injury to himself. He proceeded to acquire the means to repay that debt through burglary, only to be caught in the act by the elderly owner. At this point my client reacted in fear and panic, attempting to quieten the lady and inadvertently smothering her. He most bitterly regrets that action and begs Your Lordship to take that into account.'

Westing thanked him and asked the clerk to read out the statements from the accused and witnesses, which he duly did. The Judge then asked and received the acknowledgement by Brookland that Bracewell had no past criminal record.

He then informed the court that he and the clerk would confer in his chambers for fifteen minutes, after which time he would pass sentence.

❖

As soon as the door closed behind him, Henry Westing took off his wig and dropped it onto the table beside the door. Then he slumped into the chair by the unlit fireplace. His clerk lowered himself into the chair opposite.

'God, Leo, this is a miserable business!'

'That it is, your Honour.' said Leo Wayt. He had been Clerk of the Court for sixteen years, fourteen of them to Henry Westing. He knew how stressed Westing felt; the weight of the responsibility and the prick of conscience increased with every capital case Westing tried.

Bless the man; much as he hated it, he felt obliged to ensure the guilty got the best advice, and the most balanced trial the law could give. He was thorough in his preparation and made an effort to get to know the police and barristers in the district so he might ensure fairness extended to the defence and the prosecution cases both.

'Is there anything we've forgotten, Leo? Anything I can do to avoid that...thing?' He gestured to the square of black silk resting on the desk.

Wayt shook his head. 'He confessed freely to a stranger to gain favour, and again to the police at the station. He pleaded guilty, and although he admits he feels bad, he didn't turn himself in the next morning and lied to the police until caught. He even wrote the newspaper article after the murder!'

Westing nodded. 'Yes, I've noted those points too. And the only point I can give in his favour is that he brought no weapon with him, but used what was immediately to hand.'

'He could have left when discovered, allowed her to call the police for burglary and attempted theft.'

'Yes, Leo, he could have stopped gambling earlier, or not at all. I've been through all those scenarios too. It isn't that the crime isn't worthy of punishment, but that the punishment is, in reality, a new crime! It leaves no room for restitution, even a second-best one. He robbed an elderly lady of a few more peaceful years after she gave so much pleasure to her audiences, as well as charity work when her ballet days were behind her. He ended that pleasure for her too. He upset the lady caring for her, his own sweetheart. His punishment will add more to her pain, that is certain. A gaol cell would have been kinder for her sensibilities. Her nephew may feel his inheritance is tainted...'

'His wife may not feel the same way,' Wayt interrupted sarcastically.

'Leo, that is not helpful. Probably true, but not helpful. But you are right. I have to follow the law.'

Westing stood up, walked to his desk and retrieved the silk 'cap.' He stared at it for a moment, then stuffed it in his robe and turned around.

'Leo,' he said, 'Mr Bracewell's days are now officially numbered.'

❖

Brookland looked at his watch. Collins noticed the gesture and assumed Brookland was impatient for the sentence.

'I don't think they'll be long, sir. The Judge has to ensure he hasn't missed anything important. Westing has a reputation for being thorough and fair.'

'Yes, Bob, I know Henry Westing. Leo Wayt too. Bracewell will get a fair shake. That wasn't what I was worried about.'

'Oh?'

'I was wondering how Bracewell feels.' Collins looked at him in surprise. 'Oh.'

'I keep thinking that he must wonder how he came to be here.' Brookland turned to his colleague. 'I don't mean the events of the past few days. I mean how he set foot on the wrong path.'

Collins opened his mouth to speak, then closed it. 'His father was a criminal.'

'His adoptive parents weren't.'

'The Bracewells? You checked on them?' Collins seemed surprised.

'Enough to know they were 'upstanding citizens.' Brookland said wryly.

'They're dead now. Car accident.'

'Precisely. Their influence ended when James started his National Service. That's when he picked up more than just military discipline.'

'We've all been through that process since the war. We haven't all become criminals.' Collins pointed out.'

'True. Is that because we had law-abiding parents or the absence of a bad influence?' queried Brookland.

Collins thought for a moment. 'Perhaps both?'

Brookland nodded. 'Bob, I'm not trying to excuse his decisions on his background, and I'm no psychologist, but something in him chose to take one chance after another without thinking through the cumulative consequences. We all know some coppers are bent; they've been exposed to both the lawful and the unlawful ways of achieving goals. What can we as lawgivers do to make choosing the right path the easy decision?'

'Learn from the reasons given?' Collins asked.

'Or provide more alternative paths to take? Why didn't Bracewell ask for help with his gambling debt?'

Collins brightened. 'Pride? Embarrassment? The idea that he had to solve his own problems by himself?

Brookland grinned. 'Exactly. And I have an idea about that.'

❖

Precisely fifteen minutes after closing behind him, the chamber door opened, and the clerk appeared, followed by Judge Westing. 'All rise,' intoned Wayt. He stood beside Westing, who had seated himself once more in the Judge's chair. Westing took the cap from his pocket and laid it on the bench. He addressed Bracewell, who once more stood before him in the dock.

'James Bracewell, we have heard the evidence in the case against you. We have heard that you broke into the home of an elderly lady, with the intent to rob her, which you proceeded to do. On being surprised by this lady, you smothered her with her own cushion, leaving her for dead and exiting, with her possessions, back the way you came in. You had already tricked your friend into lending you his motorcycle to use in this endeavour, your own vehicle having a punctured tyre. You spent the weekend trying to sell the vase with no success, nor did you locate the man who might buy it from you, your father. When you finally returned the motorcycle, you had, by association, made your friend an accomplice to your crimes.'

'We have heard that your early life was difficult, owing to your father's criminal ways, but that you were adopted by good people and given the advantage of a good home. You had a job and no criminal convictions until the night of the murder. You threw away your good name when you defaulted on your gambling debts and took the cowardly remedy of theft and murder to prevent your own misfortune at the hands of other criminals. You intended to flee the country, and even then, your own poor sense of integrity tempted you to take employment with a man you thought to be a mobster. The only time you have shown good sense was in confessing to your actions.' Westing's expression turned grave, and his voice took on a firm timbre.

'James Bracewell, you have confessed to the charge of murdering Dora Jenkins. Do you have anything to say before sentence is passed upon you?'

Bracewell stood still, his face pale and his eyes dull. He swallowed and spoke evenly. 'No, your honour.'

The clerk took up the black 'cap', placed it upon the Judge's bewigged head, and stepped back. The Judge then intoned the words which had been known to rattle the most steadfast of murderers and cause some to weep.

'The sentence of this court is that you will be taken from here to the place from whence you came and there be kept in close confinement until Monday, the 27th of July 1953, and upon that day that you be taken to the place of execution and there hanged by the neck until you are dead. And may God have mercy upon your soul.'

Brookland and Collins took a late lunch before returning to the station. They had said good-bye to the Judge and Leo Wayt and exchanged a few words with Eve Gillespie and Edward Jenkins before making their way through the local journalists gathered to report on the sentencing for their respective papers. Several had tried to catch Brookland as he made for the door to the building; he politely asked them to leave the family and Nurse Gillespie alone, for which consideration he agreed to give a brief statement for each paper from his office in the station, followed by the official public statement from the Assistant Chief Constable when it was announced. Thankfully, this was accepted, and the two men were allowed to leave without further attention.

Brookland hurried his Sergeant to a nearby pub and ordered sandwiches and beer for both. Then they took their plates and glasses to a corner bench where Brookland quietly told Collins about the phone calls he had made and the conversations with senior officers.

Collins listened with interest and no small measure of surprise as Brookland revealed his side project in more detail.

'Bob, I can see by your face that my actions were unexpected, coming out of the blue like this. Do you approve?'

Collins nodded, 'Yes, yes I do. I just didn't expect you to, well, take it seriously enough to jump in like this. Did the DCS really like what you suggested?

'He did. And it doesn't hurt that his mother is a rather vocal advocate of the Howard League with the ear of the Met's top brass. He's hoping to make himself a good candidate for promotion.'

'What about the Station Commander?'

'He's in agreement too. He's seen his share of constables with ambitious wives and sweethearts.

'Anything I can do to help?' Collins asked.

'Just keep your eyes and ears open, Bob. I know you have the trust of those at the station; if they come to you with questions, tell them what they need to know.'

Collins nodded and finished his beer.

CHAPTER TWENTY

"Murderer of Dora Jenkins sentenced at Deneborough Assizes

by *Wringford Gazette and Echo* reporter

James Bracewell, aged 23, was yesterday sentenced to hang for the murder of Dora Jenkins of Lower Broadwood at the Assize Court in Deneborough. Judge Henry Westing pronounced sentence after a short hearing; Bracewell had previously admitted the charge and was therefore not tried before a jury. The sentence is to be carried out at Wandsworth Prison on Monday, July 27th at 9 am."

-Wringford Gazette and Echo

When Brookland arrived at the station on Tuesday morning, he was greeted by Constable Dale warning him he had several telephone memos on his desk. Brookland thanked him and headed first into his office to retrieve the notes then, still reading, to find Sergeant Collins in his corner of the Incident Room. Collins looked up and grinned at Brookland's fistful of paper.

'Morning, sir. You found them, I see.'

'You knew about these?' Brookland waved the notes.

'I think they took you at your word.'

Brookland sighed. 'Do we have anything new to investigate?'

'Nothing very serious. A burglary and a couple of minor thefts. They're all in hand.'

'Very well. I'll attend to these.' Brookland turned and left. Then he turned back briefly.

'Anything come down from the brass about the Bracewell sentence?'

'Not yet, sir. Your chance to get in first.' Collins said cheekily. Brookland wagged a finger in reprimand and left.

Seated at his desk, Brookland drew a sheet of blank paper towards him and began to think. After a long pause, he began to draft a formal statement for the press, repeating the message with slight variations for each paper, to give the impression each was personally crafted for the newspaper concerned. An hour later he picked up the telephone and dialled the first number. Thirty minutes later, he was left with only one name to call: Ed Delaney, editor of the *Wringford Gazette and Echo*. Brookland put the receiver down with a sigh and leaned back in his chair to gather his thoughts.

He deliberately left the call to Delaney until

last, not sure what to say until he dialled the editor's number. He needn't have worried; Delaney must have anticipated his call and planned his own piece. Brookland was grateful for the editor's formality. He had liked the man and sensed a hint of responsibility for his employee's actions. And Brookland was in part responsible for the consequences of those actions.

Delaney must have been of the same mind; he had framed his questions carefully, had known his man was in the wrong, no axe to grind. Somehow, that made Brookland feel less comfortable, but he answered Delaney as honestly as he could, giving him the quote he sought.

'May I ask a question of you in turn?' Brookland requested of Delaney.

'Of course, Chief Inspector. What do you wish to know?'

'What did you see in James Bracewell that made you give him a chance?'

Delaney laughed; his slight brogue becoming more discernible.

'Well, I liked what he wrote; he had a good solid command of the written language and had good instincts for what made a newspaper story. He was utterly charming when he wanted to be, to get a scoop. He turned up at my office one day with a fistful of typed, unpublished stories he'd written about things he'd seen and heard and I hired him part-time on the spot. It was obvious that he had a flair for the dramatic, and would stick with an assignment until he was satisfied it was done. I had him work alongside regular reporters for some months, learning the business. Sometimes he seemed blinkered, though, as if he saw only one angle, one point of view. Other times he was open to following whatever I suggested. However, he was always eager to learn, absorbed what everyone told him and always managed to find a way to get the story we asked of him, even if that meant he was a little late getting his copy in. I bent the rules on deadlines several times. I just thought that was his way; everyone does things a little differently, and he didn't take advantage of it. Other times he turned in his copy early, so I let it pass. I really had no idea he was gambling so heavily; he gave no hint of his private life, although he did tell me about his short stint in prison after nation service.'

'Yes, he told us as much. A fight developed in a pub over Bracewell's decision to pull out of a planned whiskey robbery. The other party tried to talk him back into it with a liberal amount of alcohol. A dust-up resulted in a few days in gaol for both parties, courtesy of the local Magistrate.'

'A robbery? He said it was over a girl!'

'The Magistrate thought so too. We pressed Bracewell on the point after we'd checked out that part of his statement. He explained he'd made a few extra pounds while in the army stores and another soldier got onto it, wanted to try something more lucrative. Bracewell had the sense to demur, but the other man kept pushing. It finally ended with the short gaol sentence, but they both pretended it was over a girl.'

'I said he was imaginative,' Delaney said ruefully. 'Anyhow, I started him off interviewing undertakers for obituaries. He soon found a way to interview the deceased's relatives, the vicar, the local publican or shopkeeper and delivered an obit that would have done the Lord Mayor proud! Unfortunately, that doesn't do much for our circulation figures, so I put him on local events, like the flower show over at Hawford. Did you read it, Chief Inspector?' Delaney spoke with a touch of pride.

'Yes, Mr Delaney, I did, and I concur with your sentiment. I'm sorry things ended the way they did.'

'So am I, Chief Inspector. I wish he'd explained his situation more fully; I must carry some of the blame for refusing to advance his wages when he requested it.'

'I doubt it would have made much difference. A week or two, perhaps. He was in too deep by then.'

'Yes, he was. But I like to think we might have put our heads together and thought of something better than his own solution to the problem. I'll have to keep a closer eye on my other reporters and hope I can be a better employer to them than I was to James.'

Brookland smiled. 'I too had the same thought about my own men. Good day, Mr Delaney.'

'Good day, Chief Inspector, and thank you.'

"Murderer of Dora Jenkins to hang
by *Wringford Gazette and Echo* reporter

The Midfordshire Police have issued the following statement after the sentencing of James Bracewell, 23, for the murder of Dora Jenkins on June 6th of this year. Detective Chief Superintendent Elden Marshall said yesterday, 'The murderer of Dora Jenkins, former ballet dancer with the Royal Ballet, has been sentenced to hang following his confession to the murder. Sentence will be carried out at Wandsworth Prison on Monday, 27th of July.'

Chief Inspector Brookland, in charge of the investigation, had this to say:

'A young man in the early stages of a promising career took the life of a much-loved former ballet dancer living out her life in peaceful surroundings at her home in Lower Broadwood. His motive was theft to pay off a gambling debt. His victim, who had treated him with kindness, was in turn, treated cruelly and deprived of her life. His panic at being discovered in the act of burglary led him to an act of violence. Two lives were lost because of his fear of being discovered during the commission of a lesser crime.' Further comments came from a local representative of the Howard League for Penal Reform who suggested that it was '...past time to end capital punishment as this barbarous sentence once again showed it was not the deterrent to homicide that its supporters illogically believed.'"

-Wringford Gazette and Echo

Brookland, having spent the previous day talking to the press, noted with some dismay that today would apparently be spent dealing with members of the public as a further consequence of DCS Marshall's briefing. A small but steady trickle of visitors to the station on one pretext or another included the aforesaid Howard League representative, a Mrs Daphne Erwin, who sought Chief Inspector Brookland's support in her endeavours. Brookland politely but firmly rebuffed her invitation to talk at the League's next meeting in Deneborough next month, pointing out that his position prevented him from offering personal opinions on political matters, but that privately, he wished her well in her efforts. Another life lost, he reminded her. Mrs Erwin, a stout, middle-aged woman who might have been a success on the local town council for the forcefulness of her character, thanked him and departed in good spirits. She was followed in due course by the appearance of the victim's nephew, Edward Jenkins, who, having attended the sentencing on Monday had come to thank Brookland for his efforts. Brookland acknowledged his thanks, assured him of his continuing efforts to return the stolen property in due course, and hoped for his continued good health. Jenkins, too, departed in a lighter mood than before. Brookland idly wondered if he should charge for his restorative services.

His next visitor was less welcome.

Brookland was finishing his afternoon cup of tea when Constable Bowers knocked on the open door of his office.

'Afternoon, Bowers. What is it?'

'Sir, Trevor Jarman is in the station, asking for you.'

Brookland frowned. 'Did he say what he wanted?'

'No, sir.'

'All right, send him through. And then ask Sergeant Collins to step this way, but remain out of Jarman's sight.'

'Yes, sir.'

Bowers disappeared and a few moments later footsteps echoed along the passage.

Trevor Jarman appeared in the doorway, the slight smirk on his face telling Brookland it wasn't because he was doing his civic duty and reporting something suspicious.

Brookland stood and indicated a chair. 'Good afternoon, Mr Jarman. If you've come to report a crime, the front desk is the usual place to go.'

Jarman, still smirking, took the proffered seat, and Brookland resumed his. A slight tap indicated Collins was also present.

'So, Mr Jarman, why are you here?'

'It's concerning Mr MacDonald's debt.'

'His contract with you isn't binding. You know that. What is this really about?' Brookland sensed this wasn't the reason for the man's visit.

'I have some information that might be of interest to you.' Jarman smiled at him. Brookland's intuition told him this was going to be unpleasant.

'And that would be...?'

'One of your officers tried to arrange a loan with me. The amount is small, but in light of previous events, I felt inclined to refuse. However, I felt I should bring it to your attention.'

'Which officer?'

'My assistant was given the name Constable James Bracewell.'

Brookland stared at the man for a moment, then burst out laughing. Jarman frowned. 'I don't understand, Chief Inspector. What is so amusing?'

Brookland wiped the tears from his eyes as Collins eased himself into the room from his spot close to the doorway.

Brookland became serious again. 'Mr Jarman, haven't you read the newspapers recently?'

'Newspapers? No, I've been away... on business, the past few weeks. Why?'

'Because James Bracewell is the adoptive name of our murderer, Hamish MacDonald. He's due to hang soon. So, whatever you're selling, we're not buying. And you should know somebody is playing you.'

Jarman looked from the Brookland to the now-smiling Collins. 'What? They're the same person? Then who...?'

Collins' expression flickered for a split-second as something fell into place. 'Mr Jarman, does the name 'Billy Hill' mean anything to you?'

Jarman blanched and shot to his feet. 'Oh, God,' he said. 'Never mind. Good day, gentlemen.' He rushed out of the door and ran for the station entrance without another word.

Brookland and Collins were still chuckling as they collected their coats and prepared to leave for the day.

❖

The next morning, Joseph Brookland called together his detectives along with the uniformed officers into the operation room once the station quietened. He watched their faces for a moment as they saw the Station Commander, Inspector Chris Williams, seated in a chair at the back of the room.

Then, in a measured voice, he began.

'You have all heard how our unfortunate killer set himself on the inevitable path to prison by incurring gambling debts which he could not pay, thus bringing himself into the orbit of ruthless men.' Some of his men, suspecting where this talk was leading, began to shift their feet and glance downwards. Brookland paused for a moment and continued. 'Yes, I see your reactions,' he said, 'and I want you to take particular notice of what I am about to say. It is tempting to try to win extra money, and all of us at some time or other have been certain we would never do anything rash or illegal to cover our losses. No doubt James Bracewell thought the same at one time. However, he did just that, and he made a worse decision to cover the earlier mistakes, until, well, you all know how that will end. I do not want anyone in this station making any of those mistakes.' He paused and watched his men stiffen in anticipation of his next words.

'That is why I wanted to speak to you all. The Station Commander and I...,' He turned briefly to include Williams, who nodded, 'have decided that If any of you find yourself in financial difficulty, we want you to come and tell us in confidence immediately before you try to find a way out of your problems. We will not judge you, or put it on your record, although I might call you a bloody fool—' His men all laughed; some still looked thoughtful, but most appeared relieved,'—but we will do our best to help you find a way out of your difficulties. Just don't try to do this alone out of pride or fear of losing your job. It's better that we know, then we can work together to find a solution, just as we do to catch our villains. We have options as senior officers, and our fees will be non-financial.'

His men laughed once more; most had first-hand knowledge of the perks of being senior officers through carrying out car-washing and running personal errands for their bosses.

'Is that understood?' Brookland asked when the laughter and comments had died down.

The men all nodded and responded, 'Yes, sir,' now that they knew they were not about to be punished for some unknown infraction of police procedure.

'Pass the word to those who are elsewhere today and think about what I've said. Dismissed.'

The men left the room to return to their duties, go on patrol or to discuss Brookland's words amongst themselves.

Collins smiled to himself as he, too, left the room.

❖

James Bracewell wasn't unaware of the irony of the situation. Here was a journalist writing his own last words to his editor, his estranged father and his lady friend. And all under the watchful eye of the prison warder. He stared at the blank sheet for a moment and began.

Dear Ed,

Let me say first that I agree with you: I know I am a disappointment to you. You warned me about my betting; I agreed and still placed those bets. To say now that I wished I had not is an understatement; it has led to my ruin just as you predicted, although I doubt when you said it that you had two deaths in mind. I want to thank you for trying to make a reporter out of me; despite what you may think I have always respected and admired you; I had intended to dedicate my first novel to you - another piece of unfinished business I'm afraid. Ed, one further favour if I may; I have enclosed my own account of the murder so you can print the truth. I'm sure I can count on you to see it go to press. Let Harry Brent take credit for it. He got me the details I needed when I couldn't and I know he was puzzled by my dedication to writing those pieces about my own actions; he thought it was loyalty to Miss Jenkins or admiration or something like that. I hope he knows how sorry I am for lying to him about my real motivation. He should get the credit for his pieces too.

James Bracewell, Reporter.

A few minutes later, Bracewell started a new sheet.

Dear Father,

I write this from the condemned cell, under the

watchful eye of the warders. By the time you receive this, I will be dead. I was on my way to meet you when the police arrested me for murder. I am sorry to have missed you, especially since we will never see each other. It seems we were fated not to meet again. I want to thank you for your efforts to have the Bracewells adopt me; years later they told me how much that pained you and I regret that I let you all down by failing to live up to your hopes and theirs; I had high hopes for myself too, but I let my stubbornness lead me into debt and foolish, impulsive decisions. Perhaps we will meet again one day, in a better world. I'll try not to make the same mistakes up there too.

Your son, Hamish.

Bracewell lay down on his bunk for an hour before writing to Eve Gillespie.

My Dear Eve,

Please believe me when I say how bitterly I regret the pain I have caused you. My impulsive act betrayed your trust and ended the life of a gentle and generous elderly lady. I see it all so clearly now. Why did I not see how foolish was my plan? I thought I was taking a trinket that would not be missed for weeks or months, an action to save myself from defaulting on a gambling debt. I never thought it would lead to the gallows! My vice has led to two deaths and disillusionment. What a bitter end to an otherwise hopeful life! Forgive me for my self-pity; staring at these walls has finally made me see the truth; how ironic that my reason for not dis-closing my gambling debt to you was to spare you the knowledge of my flaws. Now you know them in full. I have asked Chief Inspector Brookland to bring you this letter; I do not want you to hear of my death from a stranger.

Goodbye, my sweet Eve,

James.

EPILOGUE

"James Bracewell hanged at Wandsworth Prison

by *Wringford Gazette and Echo* reporter

The killer of an elderly spinster yesterday met his maker. James Bracewell, also known as Hamish MacDonald, was sentenced to hang for the murder of Dora Jenkins of Lower Broadwood. That sentence has today been carried out at Wandsworth Prison. May his soul rest in peace."

-*Wringford Gazette and Echo*

Brookland read the newspaper article twice before handing it to his Sergeant. Collins had just put his head around his boss's doorway to inform him of a development in a new case when Brookland called him inside to see for himself the article in question.

Collins read the piece and frowned. 'Is that another reporter's work? Because it reads like Bracewell's style.'

'I thought so too. Let's find out.' He picked up

the telephone receiver and dialled a number from the file on his desk. A few moments later, the call connected, and Brookland was once more speaking to the editor of the *Wringford Gazette and Echo*.

'Mr Delaney? Chief Inspector Brookland, Wringford CID. I read the piece about James Bracewell's hanging. Could you tell me who wrote it?' He paused, and then, 'Yes, I thought as much. Thank you. He did? May I see a copy? Yes, thank you, that would be helpful. Goodbye.'

Collins tilted his head in query and Brookland laughed. 'We were correct. Bracewell did write his own hanging announcement!'

Collins gaped. 'That took some nerve. What a thing to do!'

'His editor said he didn't want his death to be mishandled or made out to be anything significant.'

Collins shook his head. 'If I found myself in that position, I don't think I'd be worried about my reputation or whether it was mishandled. Perhaps he fancies himself as some kind of gangster after all. A Jimmy Cagney character, wanting his death to be a warning, not a martyrdom.'

'Perhaps, said Brookland. 'Or perhaps just a young man who never really threw off a bad parent's influence on his ambitions. Either way, let's take this to the pub and raise a glass to the two departed souls and to those they left behind to mourn them.'

THE END

Printed in Great Britain
by Amazon

18745977R10149